HAUNTED

BARNSLEY

HAUNTED
BARNSLEY

Richard Bramall & Joe Collins

*We would like to dedicate this book to the good people of Barnsley,
our long-suffering wives who put up with many late nights while we wrote
it, and all the friends who we dragged along in the freezing cold on our ghost
hunts over the years. Also, our warmest thanks and deepest respect must go
to the departed souls who returned from the dead and kept us up late into
the night. Without all of your help, there would be no book to write.*

First published 2012

The History Press
The Mill, Brimscombe Port
Stroud, Gloucestershire, GL5 2QG
www.thehistorypress.co.uk

© Richard Bramall & Joe Collins, 2012

The right of Richard Bramall & Joe Collins to be identified as the
Authors of this work has been asserted in accordance with the
Copyrights, Designs and Patents Act 1988.

British Library Cataloguing in Publication Data.
A catalogue record for this book is available from the British Library.

ISBN 978 0 7524 6445 9

Typesetting and origination by The History Press
Printed in Great Britain

Contents

	Acknowledgements	6
	About the Authors	7
	Introduction	8
	A Short History of Barnsley	9
one	Birdwell	11
two	Carlton	13
three	Central Barnsley	14
four	Cundy Cross	18
five	Darfield	20
six	Elsecar	24
seven	Gawber	28
eight	Goldthorpe	37
nine	Grimethorpe	38
ten	Hemingfield	40
eleven	Hickleton	42
twelve	Higham	45
thirteen	Hoyland	46
fourteen	Kendray	49
fifteen	Lundwood	52
sixteen	Monk Bretton	56
seventeen	New Lodge	58
eighteen	Newmillerdam	59
nineteen	Penistone	60
twenty	Royston	72
twenty-one	Silverstone	73
twenty-two	Skelmanthorpe	75
twenty-three	Stainscross	76
twenty-four	Stairfoot	77
twenty-five	Tankersley	82
twenty-six	Thurgoland	84
twenty-seven	Thurnscoe	87
twenty-eight	Wombwell	89
twenty-nine	Worsbrough	91

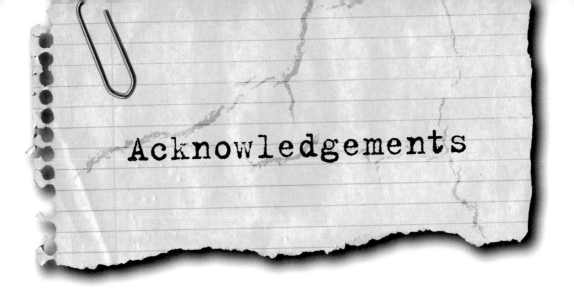

Acknowledgements

We would like to thank the following people and organisations for their contributions to this book: Judy King; Andy Beecroft; Barnsley Central Library; Heidi Cook; Carol Moore; Jan Harris; Leeanne Clegg; Graham Hawks; Chris Hepple; *Yorkshire Times*; Steve Sylvester from Hoyland Lowe Stand Trust; the Tudor family; Graham Noble; and Jim Lightfoot.

Richard Bramall and Joe Collins.

About the Authors

From an early age, Richard experienced a number of unexplainable apparitions – some of which were terrifying. These were treated as imaginary friends by his family; despite becoming less frequent as he grew older, the sightings continued into his early teens. Consequently, he started to research reported sightings in the Doncaster area to see if others had had similar encounters. To feed his hunger to prove the existence of life after death, Richard founded the Rotherham-ghosts.com website in January 2004, where he could share information with others and see who came forward with their own reports.

Due to a traumatic paranormal experience as a child that was dismissed by parents and teachers alike, Joe felt compelled to provide evidence that what he had witnessed during this episode was not a 'dream' or his 'imagination'. This sparked his obsession with the supernatural. He read every book on the subject and searched endless websites, tracking down recorded sightings of ghosts to help him find evidence.

In a twist of fate, the pair finally met in 2006 when their obsessions with the paranormal collided. They met through a mutual friend, Gary Crompton, who was a former college classmate of Joe's and had since being working alongside Richard in a paranormal group. They soon realised that their paths had crossed many times before. Through having the same interests, they had unknowingly swapped a large amount of information through third parties and forums, and had each read and investigated the reports published by the other. They have worked together since 2006, collaborating their information to publish in this book.

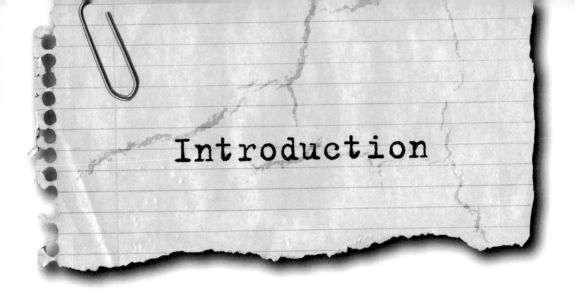

Introduction

The British Isles are arguably amongst the most haunted locations in the world, and Barnsley plays its part in this. Over the years, we have amassed a vast amount of knowledge and experience on the reported hauntings around Barnsley – and where better to share it all than in a book, which people can refer to in years to come. Contained herein are some of the reported sightings and stories from ordinary people who believe that they have had an extraordinary experience. This book is aimed at everyone interested in the legions of phantoms that inhabit Barnsley's homes, pubs and highways.

When we ask people if they believe in ghosts, we are often greeted by one of the following replies: 'There's no such thing!', 'There's something, but I don't know what!' or 'Yes, I have seen one!' People who have witnessed ghosts, and especially those who have been involved with demonic cases, are not always quick to reveal their true beliefs. They often feel embarrassment, humiliation or even guilt.

Unfortunately, we live in a society that seems to ridicule and dismiss paranormal reports. Some large organisations do not want the public to be privy to information on hauntings at their premises. Nor do some individuals want their best friends and closest relatives to know of their experiences – sometimes going to great lengths to cover up their encounters. We are putting a number of these accounts in print, though names and locations have been changed in order to protect identities.

Richard Bramall and Joe Collins, 2012

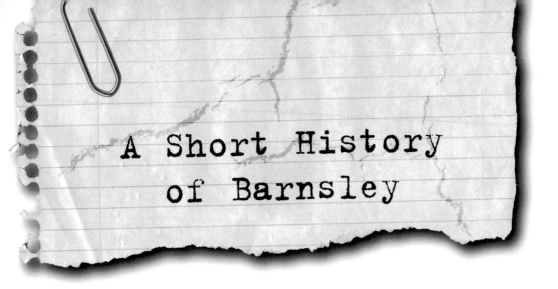

A Short History of Barnsley

The South Yorkshire town of Barnsley lies on the River Dearne. It is surrounded by several smaller settlements, which together form the Metropolitan Borough of Barnsley. Barnsley is notable as a former industrial town, centred on coal mining and glass making; a few factories still remain, notably the glassworks and coking plant. Though these industries declined in the twentieth century, Barnsley's local culture remains rooted in its industrial heritage.

The first historical reference to the town occurs in 1086 in the Domesday Book, in which it is called 'Berneslai', with a total population of around 200. The exact origin of the name Barnsley is still subject to debate, but Barnsley Council claims that its roots lie in the Saxon word Berne (for barn or storehouse) and Lay (for field). The original town (in the parish of Silkstone) developed little until the 1150s, when it was given to the monastery of St John, Pontefract. The monks decided to build a new town where three roads met: the Sheffield to Wakefield, Rotherham to Huddersfield, and Cheshire to Doncaster routes. The Domesday village became known as 'Old Barnsley', and a town grew up on the new site.

From the seventeenth century, Barnsley developed into a stop-off point on the route to Leeds, Wakefield, Sheffield and London. Traffic was generated as a result of this, causing hostelries and related services to prosper. Barnsley grew into an important manufacturing town and was a principal centre for linen weaving during the eighteenth and nineteenth centuries. However, it is most famous for its coalfields. All the pits have now closed, but the busy market town continues to thrive.

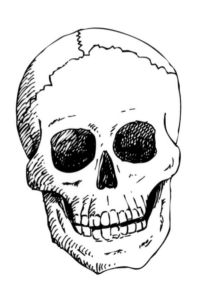

one

Birdwell

Rockleigh Furnace

Numerous strange phenomena have been witnessed at the furnace over the years. Notably, a man who was walking his dog late one evening saw light from the fiery furnace burning brightly through the trees. Walking over to take a closer look, he saw a blacksmith dressed in leather overalls, busy about his work. The smith did not acknowledge the man, he just carried on his business. Suddenly, there was a

Rockleigh furnace, when it was in use in the eighteenth century. (Authors' collection)

The Engine House, where the sound of a disembodied scream is heard. (Authors' collection)

large blast from the furnace and a bright white flash caused the man to shield his eyes for a second. When he opened them again, the scene had disappeared and all that was left was the empty ruin of the furnace.

The engine house is also said to be the epicentre of strange phenomena; supernatural lights have been seen encircling the building, and ear-piercing screams have been heard echoing throughout the woods. The sounds emanate from the bowels of the tower, where a child is said to have fallen after playing there. One brave motorist went to investigate the lights one evening, after seeing them from the roadside, but as he moved through the trees the lights vanished and a deathly silence fell about the area. As he approached the tower, he couldn't shake off the eerie feeling of being observed from a distance – he quickly returned to his car.

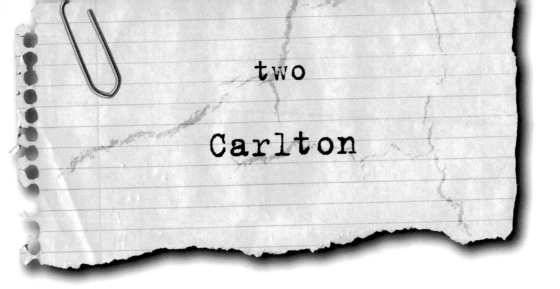

two

Carlton

Railway Line in Carlton

Carlton railway line opened in 1885 and stretched for a total of 66 miles; its name was changed in 1905 to the Hull & Barnsley Railway, even though the line never entered into Barnsley (it finished at Stairfoot). Today, the line is closed and people walk along the old tracks.

A woman out walking her dog on a crisp and frosty New Year's morning noticed another woman approaching. As they drew level, she saw that it was an elderly lady dressed in an old knitted shawl, clasping it tightly to shelter herself from the wind. The walker thought this was a little odd, due to the lady's advanced years and the remote location, but greeted the lady with a friendly 'Good morning'. The old woman returned the gesture with a kind smile, but the dog wasn't too pleased to see the old woman and dropped to the floor, cowering and crying. A little embarrassed by the dog's actions, the walker looked up at the old lady, whose smile had now changed into a sadistic and knowing grin. At that moment the woman started to fade, and disappeared right before her eyes. The dog walker still visits the area often, but has never seen the old woman again.

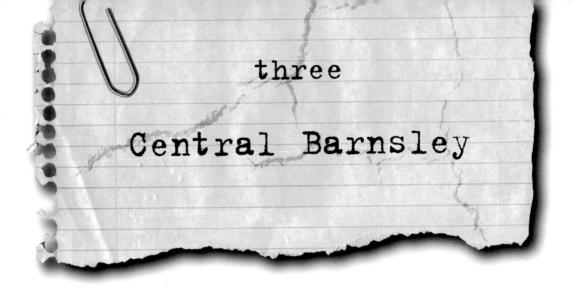

three

Central Barnsley

The Room

The Room is one of Barnsley's most infamous haunted hotspots, with strange things occurring after hours. The building was built at the turn of the nineteenth century and has passed through the hands of many landlords and ladies – very few of whom escaped without being touched by its dark secrets.

All four floors of the establishment play host to a unique haunting. The most frequently encountered is that of a lonely spinster wandering around the

The Room, where all four floors seem to be haunted. (Authors' collection)

main bar area, who is believed to be in search of a man to marry. The woman died in a tragic accident before she could find the husband of her dreams.

An old man dressed in a butcher's apron lurks in the shadows of the cellar; staff have reported that when they are changing the barrels, the man appears from the darkness and stumbles towards them reeking of gin, causing much distress.

On the second floor, footsteps have been heard on the floorboards, even though at the time the area was carpeted; and on two separate occasions a loud, clear knock has been heard on the bedroom door, rousing the sleeping occupants – who find the hallway empty.

Cries of a young lady have also been heard, but upon investigation nothing is ever found in the empty attic.

Barnsley Chronicle Offices

Barnsley's biggest newspaper offices are allegedly haunted by a weeping woman in white, and an ethereal figure, seemingly made from black smoke, which drifts from room to room. The building is said to have been built partly over the site of a former morgue, which perhaps accounts for the phenomena. It is claimed that morgues are the favourite hunting ground for demons waiting to reap the souls of the damned. Could this black entity be unaware that the site is no longer a morgue?

The Barnsley Chronicle offices, home to Barnsley's biggest newspaper. (Authors' collection)

Hedonism Nightclub

Hedonism nightclub has been a popular venue for many years, and even the loud music doesn't stop a mysterious spectre from showing up. The ghost has been seen standing on the balcony wearing a brown smock. Many clubbers and staff have reported seeing the man observing the dance floor before disappearing from view.

Oakwell Football Ground

The West Stand is the only original part of Oakwell Stadium still remaining, and the seats are the originals from the early 1900s. Staff say that if you go into the West Stand, one of the seats will fold down on its own as if someone has taken a seat. Rumour has it that this is an old fan who still comes to watch the game.

Cemetery Road

A strange figure has been spotted standing by the side of the cemetery gate. Eyewitnesses have described him as tall and thin, wearing an old top hat with a black silk ribbon and very smartly dressed. Some people believe that he only appears when a burial is imminent in the graveyard.

Barnsley Picture House

During the 1980s, an electrician was called to the building to service the emergency lighting. As he went down one of the emergency exit corridors, he shuddered; he claimed it was like walking into a freezer. Later, he met the caretaker of the cinema and asked why the corridor was so cold. The caretaker said, 'Can you feel it too?' The lighting in the corridor had all

Oakwell Football Ground as it stands today.

blown and not one of the bulbs was now working. The caretaker explained that the reason for the lights blowing was a fire that had broken out one Saturday back in 1908. Sixteen children had been killed in a crush when they went to see the novelty of moving pictures at the public hall in Eldon Street. Some of the children died in the corridor from smoke inhalation, and, ever since then, the lamps have all blown shortly after fitting. To this day the corridor remains cold, despite the heating being on full. Staff have reported hearing children's screams and smelling smoke when the building is closed.

Harberhills Road

A former resident of a terraced house just off Harberhills Road, Barnsley, reported a strange haunting to us, which had occurred eleven years ago whilst they lived there.

The first unusual occurrence was the smell of cigarette smoke, although no one in the house was a smoker. The activity slowly increased during their time there, including an incident where a small vase of flowers flew off the television set and smashed on the opposite wall. On another occasion, the resident was sat downstairs with all of the doors closed when an invisible hand poked her quite violently, causing her to jump up and spin around, only to discover that she was alone in the room. The final straw came when she was lying in bed and heard someone walking upstairs. The creaking of the floorboards stopped and started; she jumped out of bed and opened the door, but there was no one there. Disturbed by the frequency of unexplainable happenings, she moved shortly afterwards.

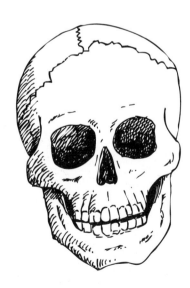

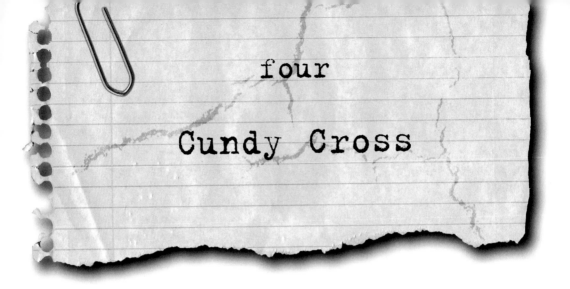

four

Cundy Cross

The Mill of the Black Monks

The Mill of the Black Monks dates back to the eleventh century. In order to provide the priory with running water, the monks redirected the course of the River Dearne; the mill was built in what was once the riverbed.

The mill stood empty for many years, boarded up and heading for ruin, until, finally, it was bought in order to renovate it into a public house and restaurant. However, having been built on the original riverbed, planning permission was flatly refused for safety reasons. Over the years the building began to sink further into the silt bed, and the only way to restore it was to raise it up and place it on a concrete raft. This massive undertaking took place in

The Mill of the Black Monks restaurant – the building was once part of the abbey. (Authors' collection)

1991 and finally the mill was restored and opened up for business as a public house and restaurant; it is still in use today, and is said to be one of the oldest and most haunted pubs in Britain.

The building is known locally as the Ale House of the Dead. The fleeting black figure of an eleventh-century monk has been seen on many occasions gliding through the grounds of Monk Bretton Priory, over the road to the old mill, before disappearing in the doorway. This phantom monk has also manifested in the shadows of the bar, and has been described as so lifelike that witnesses think it's someone in fancy dress – but their blood quickly runs cold when he disappears.

The phantom monk is not alone in haunting the site: the spirit of the old church minister has been seen lurking around the restaurant seating area known as The Granary; he is often confused as a customer, but disappears when approached.

An artist's impression of the ghost monk who haunts The Mill of the Black Monks.

Bar staff have described how unseen icy-cold grappling hands have groped and touched them in a menacing manner. Moreover, sightings of mist have been reported emerging from the outer walls of the building, before evolving into the perfectly formed incarnations of souls from the past, spanning all periods of time. These sightings include a Cavalier and a woman dressed in a habit. Upon reaching the middle of the room, they disperse back into the atmosphere.

Customers have seen small objects – such as ashtrays and glasses – move apparently of their own free will. On occasion, it is as though someone has lifted their glass and tossed it across the room; at other times as if someone has stolen their drink, sliding it across the table to an empty seat.

During our radio interview with BBC Radio Sheffield, presenter Toby Foster told us of a strange encounter he experienced whilst he was landlord of the Mill of the Black Monks. Toby recounted how one evening, after closing, he and a friend were playing cards in the bar when the sound of footsteps came from the gangway above. There were two stairways to the balcony, one to the left and one to the right. He shouted upstairs, thinking there was someone else in the building, but there was no response. So, Toby ascended one staircase whilst his friend ascended the other, blocking any escape route. But to their shock they met in the middle and discovered that they were the only two people in the building. Even though he is a sceptic, this incident still puzzles Toby.

Whether you believe in ghosts or not, the atmosphere inside the Mill of the Black Monks is something to be sampled at leisure; many fine old beams and ancient stone walls add to the character of the place, giving visitors the impression that they're back in the days when it was used as a mill.

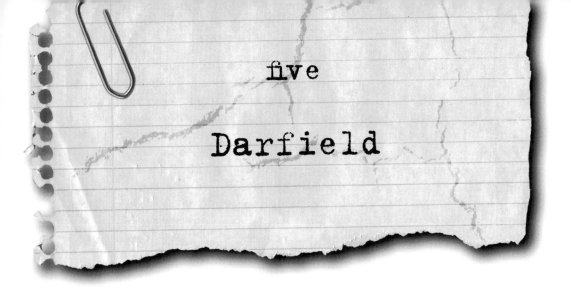

five

Darfield

Low Valley Arms

In April 2006, at approximately 1 a.m., the landlord of the Low Valley Arms public house was woken by noises coming from downstairs.

Thinking he was being burgled (the pub had recently undergone a refurbishment and he had installed several state-of-the-art flat-screen televisions), he armed himself with a large piece of lumber and went to investigate.

Low Valley Arms public house which caused a media stir when the police were called to investigate. (Authors' collection)

Once downstairs, to his surprise he found that all the TVs in the pub were switched on. His wife, who had followed him down, turned them all off, whilst he went to check the bar toilets. Swinging the ladies' toilet door open, he saw the back of a woman standing there; she wore a long, black gypsy skirt and shawl, and was facing away from him towards one of the cubicles. As he took half a step back in surprise, she turned around to reveal that the left-hand side of her face was mutilated; all the skin from the left eye socket to the throat was hanging in a flap of rotten flesh, with the eyeball protruding over the shattered cheekbone. Her muscle and teeth were exposed, and part of her jaw was missing. Terrified, and gripped with immense fear and repulsion, he bolted into the bar, where his wife called the police to report the incident.

When the police arrived they went to investigate for themselves, but instead of seeing the figure described by the landlord, all of the toilets began to flush, one at a time, by themselves. They shouted to the landlord, who also witnessed this. Although in a state of shock, he didn't want a fuss – but the police explained that due to them also witnessing a paranormal event, they would have to fill in a report. The newspapers subsequently got hold of the story and made it public.

At that time we were active paranormal investigators, and contacted the landlord as soon as we heard the report. There was much interest from national and international media and paranormal groups, but we were the only paranormal group allowed in to investigate. On arrival, we were told that the brewery had forbidden any investigation from taking place. But the landlord did allow us to interview him and take some base readings, as we had been the first people to contact him.

This was just the beginning; more incidents took place, including barrels being moved in the cellar, bottles being smashed, and the gas pressure inexplicably failing several times. They also noticed many more cold spots, and customers would often complain about the temperature in the toilets, even though the heating was on.

The landlord was so curious that he looked into the history of the pub. He discovered that a gypsy woman from the 1800s had been murdered on the site by a farmer, after she had cursed him for blaming her for a theft from his farm. The farmer had brayed the woman with his hoe, smashing her face and killing her instantly. The landlord left the pub and it changed hands twice in quick succession, before it was demolished.

Lundhill Colliery

On 19 February 1857, nearly 200 men and boys were killed in Lundhill Colliery, near Wombwell, when a gas explosion ripped through the underground workings. Of the 214 miners who went down the pit that day, only twenty-five survived the explosion. Ninety women were widowed and 220 children were orphaned.

The blast was heard and felt miles away; when rescuers tried to go down the shaft to look for survivors, they found that the coal was alight like the fires of Hades and had to abandon any attempts at rescue. Not long after the rescue team surfaced, flames began to writhe from the shaft, illuminating the countryside around the pit. After numerous attempts to put out the fire, drastic measures were taken by diverting a stream into the shaft and flooding the colliery. It wasn't until several months later that 185 bodies were eventually recovered – but some

Lundhill Colliery – the former pit. (Courtesy of Barnsley Reference Library)

were never found amongst the devastation. Most of the deceased were buried at the church in Darfield, where a monument to the explosion still stands. The cause of the explosion was declared accidental, but an inquiry did find that there had been criminal negligence at the colliery, as they had been using naked lamps and candles instead of safety lamps. The *Derbyshire Times*, 2 May 1857, reported:

> ... such was the extreme devastation, that it was rendered impossible for any engineer to explore and report upon the state of the mine. The enquiry would have to be again further adjourned to allow time for the removing of the debris, after which two engineers would be called to speak to the state of the pit. Mr Morton, in making an application for a further adjournment, said he was of opinion that an interval of probably three weeks would be required for clearing away the falls of roof, restoring the ventilation, and recovering the bodies.
>
> The body got out of the pit on Wednesday morning was identified as that of Wm. Moore. Ann Horsfield, widow, identified him. The deceased belonged to Leicester. No more bodies will have to be viewed by the Coroner and Jury, and the bodies will be interred on being recovered. The Inquiry was then adjourned until the 21st of May.
>
> Two other bodies have been recovered, one yesterday morning, and another yesterday forenoon.

When the surrounding pits were in operation during the twentieth century, the

An artist's impression of a ghostly miner. (Courtesy of Barnsley Reference Library)

ghosts of several Victorian miners were reported. Miners often worked in fear of hearing disembodied screams whilst working there. Many of the workmen would report the sounds of cries coming from the pit seams, and dark fleeting shadows running around as if they were trying to escape. Ethereal men were also witnessed at the pit head, as if they were leaving their shift to go home; but the poor souls would never make it that far. What makes these sightings horrific is that they seem to be reliving their nightmare over and over again, and their screams of terror have made many a miner quit. On one occasion, a miner saw a burning torso emerge from a coalface, before disappearing into the opposite one. Today, the pits are all closed and many of the old sites have now been built upon; we often wonder if the inhabitants of the new buildings have witnessed the strange phenomena that once terrified the miners.

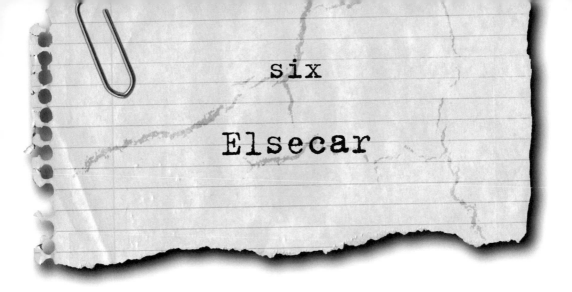

six

Elsecar

Elsecar Steam Railway

There have long been legends about a ghostly lady haunting the site, but her late-night saunter still came as a shock to the nightwatchmen one fine summer's night. It was around 12.15 a.m. when one of the security guards started his patrol,

Elsecar steam railway station as it is today. (Authors' collection)

whilst the second guard watched over him through the CCTV. As he left the guardhouse and turned the corner to his right, he noticed a glowing white shape drifting across his path from the direction of the train station. At first he thought it was a carrier bag blowing in the wind, but it was too big and its movement was too controlled; he stopped and stared hard, trying to work out what it could be. It seemed to be emitting a fluorescent blue haze. As his eyes focussed on it, he could clearly see a lady wearing a fine white-laced afternoon dress and bonnet, with a parasol over her left shoulder and a blue ribbon around her waist, tied in a bow. It was so vivid, like a hologram floating in space. He could not have been more than 15m away from the guardhouse at this time, and shouted to his colleague while

frantically waving at the security camera and pointing at the ghost.

The guard in the office heard his cry and saw his bizarre behaviour on the monitor. He stood up to go to his aid, but before he could get to the door, the first guard came running in, out of breath, saying, 'Did you see that?' The first guard explained what had happened to him; the second guard said that he hadn't seen anything through the monitors, only his colleague stopping abruptly before shouting and waving his arms. On viewing the footage, no signs of the mystery lady could be seen, only the odd behaviour of the guard – but to this day he swears that he saw a lady in white. Numerous other sightings have been reported near the railway throughout the years, always described as a well-dressed Victorian lady who melts away when approached.

The platform at Elsecar steam railway station where a ghostly figure is seen. (Authors' collection)

The Ship Inn

The Ship Inn is a small public house located just outside Barnsley in the village of Elsecar. The original Ship Inn was built in 1827 next to the main road, but the property we see today was constructed behind the original. Once this new building was finished, the original Ship was demolished to make way for an off-road parking area.

Many of the owners claim to have experienced some very odd activity during their term there. Pictures are regularly found tilted on walls, the cooker has turned on by itself, pool balls from the games room have rolled around the table on their own, and the radio has switched itself on and off when no one is present. In addition, taps in the building's toilets turn themselves on, the toilet roll is often found 'unwound' on the floor, even though it has only just been put in by the cleaners, and the building's lights appear to have a life of their own.

The customers have also experienced odd activity whilst enjoying a relaxing drink at the Ship. Several people have claimed to feel a 'presence' near them as they stood at the bar. Other patrons have been pushed from behind, even though no one is near them at the time, and most regulars have witnessed the electrics 'going crazy'. One of the landlady's granddaughters also experienced seemingly impossible phenomena when she

The Ship Inn. (Authors' collection)

stayed the night at the property. She was sat in the bar and saw her scarf moving on the table of its own accord. To her amazement, she then saw the item of clothing unfold in front of her eyes.

During our research, we uncovered some other fascinating accounts of ghostly activity at the Ship. A story that was brought up again and again concerns the apparition of a lady dressed entirely in black and sporting grey hair tied in a bun. She has been seen by many people over the years and always appears to be walking in the same area. It is said that she walks the full length of the back room and through the kitchen wall. She has also been spotted walking along the passageway and through the kitchen wall which faces the front of the building. It is said that the spirit is that of Mary Steer (also known as Polly) who used to visit the pub every night to buy a jug of ale for her husband. One night Mary did not return and a frantic search of the area was conducted but, unfortunately, Mary had fallen into the nearby canal on her way back home and drowned.

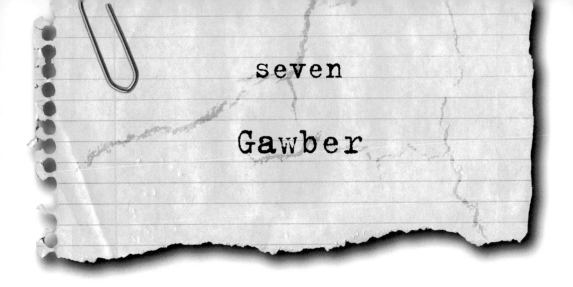

seven

Gawber

The Polish Centre

The Polish Centre on Blackburn Lane was built in the early 1800s. It was originally a school before it was changed into a private club for Polish immigrants after the Second World War. It is still trading today as a social club for the whole community.

One of the cleaners, Heidi Cook, contacted us with several reports of strange activity that she has encountered. One day, after vacuuming in the main bar area, Heidi noticed a dark shadowy man about 3ft away, who she described as being around 6ft tall, wearing a trilby, and just staring at her. Startled, she screamed and ran out of the door, as she knew that she was the only person in the building at the time. However, this wasn't the only sighting that Heidi would endure in the main bar area in the summer of 2010. On the second occasion, she looked up and saw an old man coming through the doors wearing a flat cap in a tartan design, along with a long jacket that seemed to be too big for him. The man was small in size, around 5ft, and approached Heidi, asking if he could sit down and wait for the bar to open. Seeing no problem with this, she agreed and went about her business, making small talk with the man whilst she worked. She left the bar to get something from the other room, and on her return found that the bar manager had arrived to open the pub. Heidi explained that the customer was waiting for the bar to open. The bar manager looked at Heidi and said, 'Who are you talking about?' Turning around to point the man out, she was surprised to see that there was no one there! She described the man to her manager, and was told that she had described one of the locals, named Tommy, who often waited for the bar to open in that seat – but Heidi fell faint when the landlord explained that poor old Tommy had died three years previously!

In addition to these sightings, Heidi has experienced the sound of children giggling and running around when the place is empty. On one occasion, whilst she was mopping the main hall, she was surprised to see a small boy peeping around the doorway. She described him as about five years old and wearing a blue jumper. Heidi went to check what the boy was doing, only to discover that he had vanished without a trace.

The former school which is now known locally as the Polish Centre. (Authors' collection)

The Gawber Exorcism

This is perhaps the most renowned exorcism case in English history, causing the Anglican Church to completely restructure its practice of exorcism.

In 1974, Michael Taylor lived with his wife Christine and five children in the town of Ossett, West Yorkshire. Michael was a thirty-one-year-old family man and led a seemingly ordinary life with no signs of mental illness. His only problem was difficulty finding work, which was common at this time. Despite this, the family home was filled with laughter and happiness. The family was religious but not devout churchgoers.

Barbara Wardman, a friend of the Taylors, was keen to introduce them to her Christian Fellowship organisation, led by twenty-two-year-old Marie Robinson. So,

Michael attended a service at which Miss Robinson preached. Later that evening, the Christian Fellowship group held a meeting at Michael's home, during which one of the women present, Mrs Mavis Smith, started to cry. Seeing this, Marie started shaking and stated that this usually meant the Holy Spirit was very active and his power was ready to be used in one direction. She felt this power was for Mike, because she knew that he had a bad back and was upset because he could not get a job. She wanted to make sure she was not walking outside the Lord's will by directing the power at the wrong person, so Marie decided to use the power to exorcise Mavis Smith. She knelt in front of her and practised the laying on of hands, and prayed in tongues. Surprisingly, Michael also began speaking in tongues, at which Mavis took offence and shouted that she hated Marie Robinson. Over the next twelve days Michael seemed to become infatuated with Marie, and attended all subsequent Fellowship meetings.

On 1 October 1974, during a full moon, Marie and Michael sat up all night making the sign of the cross over each other. On another evening, while Christine was out of the room, the pair fell into an embrace and kissed. Marie turned to Mike and said, 'You know all this is wrong; you know you love Chris.' Michael later said, 'She seduced me with her eyes. I can still see those eyes. I saw her standing naked before me, and I was naked …' When Christine returned to the room, Marie announced to her, 'We have won a great victory for the Lord. A miracle has happened; we have both overcome our passions.' This prompted Christine to express concern about her husband's relationship

with Marie, as she suspected that the two were becoming a little too familiar with each other and endangering her marriage.

At the next service, Michael felt an evil force taking over him and suddenly attacked Marie both verbally and physically, shouting at her in tongues and only stopping after being restrained by several other members of the congregation. The incident was quickly forgotten and he received 'absolution' at the next church meeting. However, Michael continued to exhibit bizarre behaviour, and local ministers were soon called in. The ministers recommended that an exorcism be performed to clear the troubled man of the Devil's influence.

Now believing Michael to be possessed, the group persuaded him and his wife to meet Revd Peter Vincent of St Thomas's Church in Gawber for an exorcism. Michael

St Thomas' Church, Gawber, where the exorcism was held. (Authors' collection)

and Christine were told to attend the church at midnight on 5 October. Those present included Revd Vincent (an Anglican) and his wife Sally, Revd Raymond Smith (a Methodist minister) and his wife Margaret, Donald James (a Methodist lay preacher), and John Eggins from the Fellowship group. The exorcism that followed took almost eight hours. Michael was first laid down and restrained on the floor. He was then made to confess sins, whilst having crosses pushed into his mouth and being sprinkled with holy water.

Reverend Vincent and Revd Raymond Smith claimed to have expelled over forty demons from Michael that night, including 'incest', 'bestiality', 'blasphemy', 'lewdness', 'heresy', 'masochism' and many others. They even burned the wooden cross that Michael was wearing at the time. By 7 a.m. the group were forced to stop through sheer exhaustion, but warned Michael and his wife that three demons remained: 'violence', 'anger' and 'murder'. Margaret then said she had received word from the Lord that the spirit of murder was going to break out, and advised Michael's wife to beware. Despite this, at around 8 a.m. on Sunday morning, Michael and Christine were told to go home.

By 10 a.m., police had received reports of a man running through the streets of Ossett naked and covered in red paint. They attended, but thought it might be a hoax. However, the police found Michael Taylor outside a local pub crouched in the foetal position on the footpath, covered by a blanket that the ambulance staff had issued. The first officer in attendance turned to a colleague and said, 'It's not paint it's blood, and he's slick with it.' Michael Taylor kept repeating, 'It's the blood of Satan', over and over.

Around this time, the local police inspector and sergeant discovered the body of Christine Taylor. At first they were looking for an axe or a large knife – there wasn't any. Michael, with his bare hands, had gouged out his wife's eyes, torn out her tongue and ripped her face off her skull. The police couldn't believe that a man could have done it with his bare hands.

At the trial, prosecution barrister Mr Geoffrey Baker warned the jury that they were about to hear evidence which 'would make it difficult to believe you are not back in the Middle Ages'. He went on to state that a vulnerable man had been turned into a homicidal maniac. Taylor claimed that after the exorcism he'd come to believe that his wife was possessed by demons. The Christian Fellowship group was characterised as 'a group of tormented souls who fed upon neurosis'. Mrs Wardman said, 'And with that simple act began Michael's descent' into what a court would later hear was 'a world of fear and religious mania'.

A sixteenth-century engraving of an exorcism from the Middle Ages. (Courtesy of Barnsley Reference Library)

When questioned in court about their relationship and the kiss that had seemingly caused Michael's changed behaviour, Marie said:

I suddenly glanced at Mike and his whole features changed. He looked almost bestial. He kept looking at me and there was a really wild look in his eyes. I started screaming at him out of fear. I started speaking in tongues. Mike also screamed at me in tongues … I was on the verge of death and I seemed to come to my senses. I knew that only the name of Jesus would save me and I just started saying over and over again 'Jesus'. When Chris heard me calling on the name of Jesus she started saying it too, and I believe firmly that it was only by calling on His name that I was not killed … The whole of my being just reacted completely against that, we just snapped apart. It was like a clash of wills, a clash of spirits perhaps.

When questioned, Father Peter Vincent insisted that Taylor had truly been possessed by evil spirits. Asked to comment after the trial, he said, 'I am quite convinced God will bring good out of this in His own way, however tragic it was at the time.' Revd Smith said, 'If the psychiatrist said this crime would not have been committed but for the exorcism, that seems a rather strange thing to say; people will draw their own conclusions.' Mr Ognall QC had quite a different opinion, stating:

I am aware that it is generally regarded as improper for an advocate to express any personal feeling or opinion about the case in which he is engaged. I am afraid I find it quite impossible to observe such constraints in this case. Let those who truly are responsible for this killing stand up. We submit that Taylor is a mere cipher.

The real guilt lies elsewhere. Religion is the key. Those who have been referred to in evidence, and those clerics in particular, should be with him in spirit now in this building and each day he is incarcerated in Broadmoor, and not least on the day he must endure the bitter reunion with his five motherless children.

An expert witness, consultant psychologist Hugo Milne, was asked by the judge whether the exorcism had caused the man to kill. Mr Milne said, 'It was entirely related to his trance state and his eventual killing of his wife. It caused it.' The judge accepted this view in his summing up, and made clear that the man had been a loving husband who had been exorcised into committing an unforgivable act, completely out of character. Taylor was found not guilty of the crime by reason of insanity, and was sent to the Broadmoor mental hospital for two years. This was followed by a two-year stint at a secure ward at Bradford Royal Infirmary before he was declared 'legally and clinically sane' after treatment and released. Christine's death was recorded as one of 'misadventure' at the subsequent inquest. Both Marie Robinson and Peter Vincent were pressured by the coroner as to why they had taken this course of action instead of ensuring that Michael Taylor received proper medical attention; they both claimed that they were only doing 'God's will'; neither apparently showed any remorse. No action was ever taken against them, but the Christian Fellowship run by Marie Robinson was disbanded.

After the trial, which got nationwide publicity, the Church of England published new guidelines and set up official exorcists in each diocese. The idea, of course, was to control the medieval idiocies of 'maverick' vicars. Deliverance cases must now first be referred to a panel which includes a medical psychiatrist; the Taylor exorcism remains the last acknowledged instance in an Anglican church. Following the Taylor incident, exorcism in the Wakefield diocese was banned by the bishop.

Hermit Lane

Not far away from St Thomas's Church is Hermit Lane, which has had its fair share of hauntings throughout the years.

One evening, a group of four youngsters were walking home towards Higham after being at a friend's house; it was quite late as they passed the church and headed off down the windy road home. Walking in twos, they chatted about the night's events, when all of a sudden the front two felt something punch them in the solar plexus. Winded and shocked, they both screamed out in pain; the other two ran towards

them to see what was wrong but the youths didn't stop to explain. They ran back in the direction they had come, hunched over, with their two confused friends in tow.

When they got back to the church, they explained that they had both felt a punch in the stomach at the same time. Lifting their T-shirts up, they saw clear bruise marks. Whilst they were standing outside the church gates, a further incident occurred; the two who had not been punched heard heavy breathing down their ears, as if a fifth person had joined their group.

During our investigation on this road, a local stopped and asked us what we were doing. When we explained that we were researching the alleged haunting, he informed us that the ghost of an old farm-hand travels the road late at night and, on occasion, people have reported being hit by him. In addition to this, the local told us what had happened to him early one morning back in the early 1980s.

Hermits Lane – the road where the spectre was seen. (Authors' collection)

After finishing his night shift, he had headed along Hermit Lane towards Gawber. It was about 6 a.m. and still dark. It had been snowing and, as he went up the hill through the trees, his car was struggling to keep on the road. Concentrating on his acceleration and steering, he was about halfway to the top, just after the wooded area, when he noticed someone ahead of him walking towards Gawber. He assumed it was a neighbour walking home, so he thought he'd offer him a lift.

As he approached he slowed down to get a good look, and the figure stopped and turned its head towards him. What the local man saw still terrifies him to this day. The figure had dark-coloured clothing and a burgundy-hooded full-length duffel coat, but its face wasn't human. It had the biggest, evillest grin he had ever seen – gaping like an alligator's smile, literally from ear to ear; its razor-sharp teeth were massive, like rows of razor blades too big for its mouth. And its eyes! Its eyes were as black as crude oil and bulged from their sockets.

Flooring the accelerator, he zigzagged at speed all the way to St Thomas's Church, stopping to gather his thoughts before turning the car around and going back. He had to figure out what he had just seen. He drove all the way to the bottom of the hill, scanning the roadsides and fields as he went, but nothing. It was gone, with nowhere to have gone to! He has been up and down the road thousands of times and has never seen it since.

Bark Green Road

In 1969, Jim Lightfoot and his family bought a house on Bark Green Road in Gawber. The house was in need of some modernisation before his wife and two children could move in.

Jim spent most of his spare time renovating the house alone in the early months. One day, he was removing the fireplace from the bedroom when he heard some footsteps move across the wooden floor downstairs and climb the staircase. Thinking it was someone coming to help, he called out 'Hello?' but the footsteps stopped outside the bedroom door. He paused and waited a few moments before going to look. When he popped his head out, he was surprised to see nobody there. This puzzled him; he knew he'd not imagined the footsteps.

When the house was finished, his wife and children moved into the property and settled in. After returning home from a night out, Jim went upstairs to bed while his wife stayed downstairs, having a last cigarette before she joined him. Jim climbed into bed and waited. The room was dimly lit by the bedside lamp and the light shining through the door from the hallway. Jim was just drifting off when he heard the sound of footsteps coming up the stairs. Thinking it was his wife, he said, 'Turn the light out love!' But no reply. There was someone in the room, in the darkness; he sat up to peer into the shadows. He could hear something running right from the direction he was looking, but could see nothing! Then it jumped on the bed and pinned him down to the mattress. He struggled and tried to sit up but he couldn't move; all he could feel was the flustered flapping of something like wings. He could hear the air being broken by the frantic fanning right in his face, like it was trying to lash out at him. This went on for several minutes before he finally stopped struggling, and the flapping ceased just as quickly as it had started. He jumped out of bed and ran downstairs – to see his wife still sat smoking her cigarette. She hadn't heard a thing. His wife teased him about the story, much to his annoyance.

Not long after this event, Jim and his wife were in the bedroom discussing holiday plans when they heard footsteps coming up the stairs. Jim hushed his wife: 'Listen! It's the footsteps …' They waited with bated breath. Slowly the door opened and the shimmering outline of a person glided into the room. It walked right over to Jim's side of the bed and stopped. Jim calmly said, 'What do you want?' but got no response. It simply drifted away towards the wardrobe and faded into the darkness. Jim was quite relieved that his wife had now experienced the paranormal activity, but was also a little worried.

A few days later, the couple were woken in the middle of the night by screams coming from their daughter's room. They found her in a hysterical and distraught state.

'Help Mum, help! There's an old woman in my room and she's trying to hurt me,' she pleaded. She told them that an old woman with white hair had been in her room, pulled off the covers and climbed into her bed.

Jim and his wife decided that enough was enough and decided to contact their local church – but they were more than a little alarmed when the church recommended that they have their daughter exorcised. Jim's wife was worried about this, especially since the Gawber exorcism case was currently ongoing. Moreover, one of Jim's old school friends, who had been present at the Gawber exorcism, had suffered a serious mental breakdown and had been committed to a secure psychiatric hospital. The couple spoke to a lady there who gave them a silver cross and a jewellery box bearing religious symbols. She advised them to place the items in their daughter's room. They were a bit cautious, but did as she said. However, their daughter screamed again that night. Running to her aid, they discovered that the cross had left the nail it was hung on and was now in the opposite corner of the room, and the jewellery box had been smashed into thousands of pieces. Their daughter claimed that the woman with white hair was responsible. Comforting their daughter, they looked at each other in dismay.

The following night, all seemed quiet as they went to bed. After checking on their daughter, they sat talking for a while about the recent events when they were stopped in mid-conversation by the sound of footsteps. The door was ajar and the figure made its way into the room, shimmering as it glided towards the bed. This time it sat on the bed, leaving an indentation in the covers. Jim again asked who it was and what it wanted. But the figure just seemed to lie down on the bed before disappearing.

Another night, when the couple returned home from visiting relatives, they spotted a figure standing in the upstairs window. The figure was a woman dressed in black, looking out of the window whilst holding back the curtain. When the family looked up at her, she simply put the curtain back down and walked away. Jim went upstairs but there was no one there.

Things took a turn for the worse when both Jim and his wife started to sleepwalk. Often they would wake up alone in the cellar, staring into the pitch black. Jim was beginning to think that this strange behaviour was some sort of sleep possession from the spirit that resided in the house, and wondered if it was trying to give them a message. In a bid to uncover the mystery, he dug the floor up in the cellar to see if there was anything there. However, nothing was discovered. It was only later that he realised he may have missed an important clue, for the only part of the cellar floor he had not excavated was under the coal heap that they had both been staring at when they had woken.

The cellar steps, where occupants often woke at night after sleepwalking. (Authors' collection)

Jim decided to research the history of the property and the family that once resided there. He started by asking the locals, who revealed that the family had strict Pentecostal beliefs and had lived in the property since it was first built in 1911. It was rumoured that the woman of the house had fallen pregnant but had lost the baby through miscarriage, because no one saw a child after her sudden weight loss.

Things began to make sense to Jim. He remembered that when he had been renovating the house, he had seen a lot of religious quotes written on black plaques which were fixed to the walls. One quote had stuck in his mind and his blood ran cold as he remembered it: 'The Lord Noeth those that are his.' Jim began to think that maybe the family had buried the baby's body in the cellar and that the mother's spirit could not rest until her child was buried on consecrated ground. Not knowing what to do about the situation, the family decided to sell the house. The house was soon sold and, after they had moved all of their furniture out of the property, Jim's mother went in to clean the floors before handing the keys over to the new owners. While she was there, she too heard the footsteps walking up the stairs and had a very strange sense that someone was looking over her. Not wanting to stay around and wait for the entity to emerge, she fled the house, leaving behind her cleaning supplies.

In later years, Jim's daughter started work in a department store in Doncaster. In a twist of fate, she learned that a female colleague had once lived in their old house. The woman confessed that strange things had happened to her in the house, such as disembodied footsteps and the feeling of being watched … and she would often find the cellar door wide open.

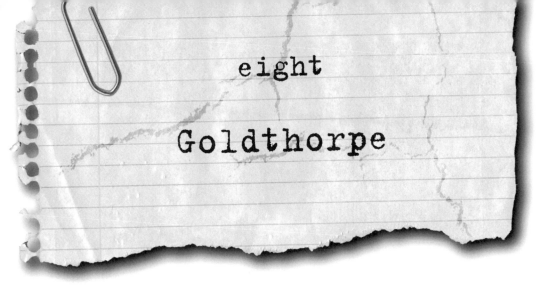

eight

Goldthorpe

Goldthorpe Colliery

In July 1985, one of the mine workers fled the coalfield after watching a pair of disembodied boots moving towards him deep underground. So scared was the man that he vowed never to return again. Like many other pit villages in South Yorkshire, Goldthorpe suffered after the collapse of the mining industry. Perhaps the boots have not been seen since.

Goldthorpe Colliery. (Courtesy of Barnsley Library collection)

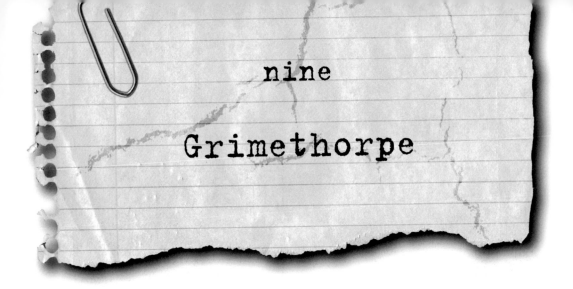

nine

Grimethorpe

Grimethorpe Colliery

Like most mines, Grimethorpe was closed not long after the strikes in the 1980s, but even back then reports of ghost sightings were common amongst the locals. The manifestation of a man wearing a grey suit startled numerous miners working underground at Grimethorpe Colliery. Witnesses described him as not wearing a helmet or lamp, and said he looked out of place in the environment. Rumours soon started amongst the workforce, who nicknamed the figure 'Charlie'. Although at first it was thought to be a hoax, the sightings continued until a number of colliers refused to visit the seam where Charlie had been seen. No clue to his identity was ever found, and Charlie remains a mystery.

An unconnected sighting was reported in 1978 by a former Grimethorpe mining engineer. He often worked alone on haulage engines in an isolated area of the pit. On one of his night shifts, he was joined by a man he didn't recognise; he just assumed the man had been drafted in from another local colliery. The worker introduced himself as Joe. They worked and chatted together for several hours, when a message came over the tannoy system for the engineer to stop the haulage and leave the site. The pit deputy informed the engineer that the belt needed shunting. The engineer said that Joe, who was still on site, could operate it without the need for him to return. The deputy looked at the engineer in confusion – he had no record of anybody else in that area of the pit; he told the engineer that no man had entered or left and, if they had, then they would have had to let him know. Besides, their only route would have been to go directly past him. The two men, along with three others, immediately went to the haulage area and found it empty. However, a shovel and a half-cleared pile of coal were in the place where he had last seen Joe working. The engineer had spent enough time with the mystery miner to give a good description. On reporting this to control, it was confirmed that nobody of this description, or of the name of Joe, had been underground.

Later, the mystery miner was identified. A man who had worked with Joe until his death in the 1940s recognised him from the engineer's description. Pit officials asked the engineer to keep quiet about the inci-

Grimethorpe Colliery. (Courtesy of Barnsley Library collection)

dent, so that other men working in the area wouldn't refuse to go down there. The family of the ghostly miner soon heard of the sighting and questioned the engineer about what he had seen. He gave them a description and recounted their conversations; the family were convinced that it was Joe whom he had been talking to.

The Red Rum

The Red Rum public house is situated on Cemetery Road, Grimethorpe, and is believed to be haunted by the spectre of a woman who died there in the last century. Doors have reportedly opened themselves for people to walk through, and cleaners and customers have both spotted a lady in a long skirt, who appears and disappears suddenly.

In 1990, one of the regulars was about to leave the pub one night, after last orders, when he saw a woman walk through the bar. Knowing that nobody could have entered the premises, and the doors were locked, he quickly described the woman to the landlady. The figure had been dressed in an old-fashioned manner, in long skirts and a cap. The landlady knew instantly that he had seen the resident ghost. There have been several similar sightings of a woman in a long skirt over the years, though her exact identity remains a mystery.

An artist's impression of the ghostly serving girl. (Courtesy of Barnsley Library)

39

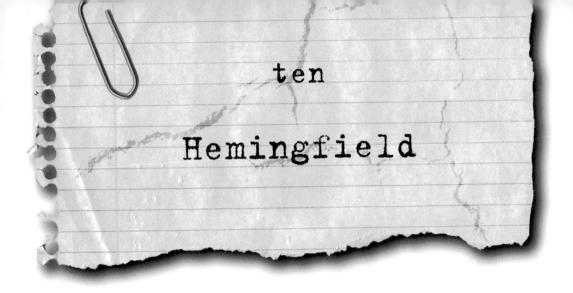

ten

Hemingfield

The Fiddlers Inn

The Fiddlers Inn, constructed in the late eighteenth century, was once the heart of the community and a second home to many of the local miners, who took a daily pint of ale within its walls. The pub began life as the Milton Arms Hotel, named after the local estate owner. Milton owned the majority of the surrounding lands and employed many of the locals. In the 1970s, however, the inn was closed for many years; it is alleged that a local girl was murdered there. Despite our research, we were unable to verify this incident. The public house reopened in the 1980s with the name Fiddlers Inn, but was renamed the Marbrook Tavern in 2001. In 2006, under new owners, the name reverted once again to the Fiddlers Inn.

Throughout the various changes, the pub never lost its air of dark secrets; no wonder then that it is reputed to be haunted by five spectres. Various landlords and patrons have reported that taps behind the bar have turned themselves on and off, and the light has been switched off by unseen hands. Shadowy figures have also been seen in the kitchen. Furthermore, some of the male regulars have seen a figure in the men's toilets, who has passed a few kind words with them and then vanished.

The following story was told to us by a man who saw our appeal for ghost stories in the Barnsley area. The year was 1971 and the pub had closed down; it stood alone, fallen from its former glory but still dominating the landscape. Like most empty buildings, it attracted the curious. The man in question asked us not to disclose his name, so for the purpose of this story we will call him Billy.

When Billy was twelve, he and several friends were walking past the old building when they noticed that one of the doors on an upstairs fire escape was wide open. The inn's broken windows were like empty eyes, beckoning them to plunder its secrets. Enticed, the group ascended the metal stairway and entered the dark building. All of the windows were boarded, blanketing the rooms with dark shadows pierced by the icicles of light which splintered through the cracks. Slowly their eyes adjusted to the gloom, giving them enough light to find their way around the building. Everyone shot off in a different direction to explore, leaving Billy in the hallway. He slowly crept along the corridor, looking into each desolate room until he reached a flight of stairs leading to a higher floor; as he put one foot on the first step, he instantly felt that someone was there, waiting for him. Cautiously, he gazed up to see the feet of a man wearing fawn-coloured trousers. At first he thought it was a neighbour coming to investigate the noise; he braced himself for a clip around the ear, but nothing. The man just stood there and stared at him. He wore a chequered sporting jacket, a deer-stalker hat … but the face! The face was blurred and looked like it was not quite of this world. Suddenly, the feeling of impending doom swept over Billy; he wanted to run, he wanted to scream to his friends for help, but he couldn't. It was as if the figure held some power over him, freezing him to the spot; they both stood motionless for what seemed an eternity, and all Billy could hear was the beating of his heart, the blood thumping inside his head. A surge of adrenaline coursed through his body. He knew he had to break its grip and run – not just for his life but for his very soul.

Billy bolted downstairs, where his friends were shouting, 'Get the hell out of here!' As he reached the bottom of the stairs, he could see light coming through the glass door that led into the main bar. He burst through the doors and ran around the bar to get out, but his escape was denied by the very figure he was running from. It just stood there, glaring down at him, motionless and silent. Billy tried to slide to a halt to avoid running right into the clutches of the figure, but, unable to stop his momentum, he lost his footing and slipped, cutting his leg in the process. Scrambling back to his feet, he raced back the way he had come to try to find another way out. This time he jumped over the bar and down the trapdoor into the dark cellar, bursting up through the cellar delivery hatch to safety. His friends were waiting for him up the street. When Billy finally caught them up, he asked if they had seen the man in the Edwardian hunting gear. They said they had not, and had only run after hearing Billy scream. Billy told us that a lot of folks don't believe him, but he still has the scar on his leg to prove it.

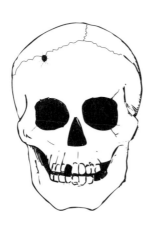

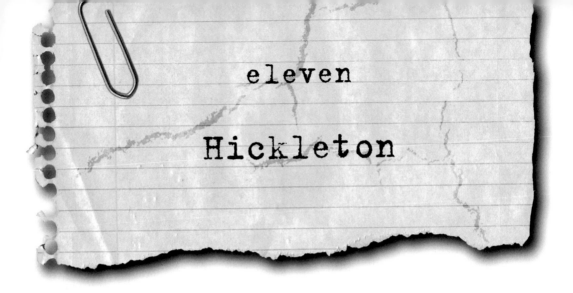

eleven

Hickleton

Hickleton Church

There has been a church at Hickleton since Norman times, but the building you see today is essentially Perpendicular in style. The church's interior was extravagantly

Hickleton church, viewed from the lychgate that houses the skulls. (Authors' collection)

furnished at the expense of the Halifax family, who were also responsible for the Victorian restoration. The church should be remembered for its long association with 2nd Viscount Halifax, and for the three skulls he so provocatively displayed at the lychgate.

Legend has it that the three skulls belonged to men who were hanged for the crimes of rustling or witchcraft (depending on which version of events is true). They were hanged at the gallows on the village's Hangman's Lane before being displayed in gibbets on the boundary as a warning to others. When the rotten remains were taken down, the corpses were each decapitated and their skulls were imprisoned into the church lychgate, with the chilling words 'Today for me, tomorrow for thee' inscribed into the stone beneath.

The second version is that the skulls were of three African slaves belonging to the Halifax family, who were caught practising voodoo. They were beheaded and buried in the churchyard in unmarked graves. The family is said to have used the skulls as a warning to others.

The skulls which are embedded in the stone archway. (Authors' collection)

Local legend says that if you visit the lychgate on All Hallows Eve at 3 a.m. – the witching hour – you can hear the skulls mumbling and reciting a curse. More recently, one of the skulls was stolen by what is believed to be a local group of occultists, perhaps in a bid to obtain the secrets of the curse and assist with their black art practices. To date, the skull has not been found and has been replaced by a replica.

Hickleton Crossroads

Hickleton crossroads is reputed to be a place of high paranormal activity. It was common practice to bury witches and suicides at crossroads. Additionally, a gibbet was sometimes erected there as a warning not to break the law in that parish. It is believed that a mighty gibbet once stood at Hickleton.

A cyclist travelling from Barnburgh towards the crossroads at Hickleton reported seeing a man on horseback cantering towards the crossroads. As they met at the intersection the horse reared, revealing to the cyclist that the horseman was wearing a riding cape and tricorn hat. Before the cyclist had time to make sense of what he was seeing, both rider and horse dissolved into thin air.

In 1977, a lorry driver reported having to brake hard at the junction when the horseman suddenly appeared in the middle of the road from nowhere. It vanished just as quickly, leaving the driver astounded. These are just a couple of the many reports concerning the mysterious horseman of the Hickleton crossroads.

Hickleton Hall as it stands today. (Authors' collection)

Hickleton crossroads where the figures are seen. (Authors' collection)

The Wicker Men

In the early 1990s, a couple were travelling home from Doncaster towards Hickleton. As they approached the junction, the clock struck 3 a.m. They slowed down to turn the corner opposite the monument near the church, when they noticed two geriatric men dressed in long white nightgowns and matching nightcaps. One of them was seated in an old wicker wheelchair which was being pushed by the other; both stared at the car as it passed by. The couple thought this was odd, and wondered if the old men had strayed from a residential home. They decided to stop the car and check on them, but, as they stepped out, to their amazement the two old gentlemen waved and disappeared.

Hickleton Hall

Hickleton Hall is a splendid eighteenth-century house standing behind St Wilfred's Church. Today it is a nursing home. Cleaning staff swear that they have felt a presence there, and have heard children singing nursery rhymes. On one occasion, children were heard playing in an empty upstairs room and calling out, 'Coming ready or not!' After staff had closed the door and returned to their duties, children's laughter was heard, as if they were playing hide-and-seek with the cleaners. Staff don't seem to be too fazed by this and, when the voices are heard, they often joke amongst themselves, 'It's those bloody kids again.'

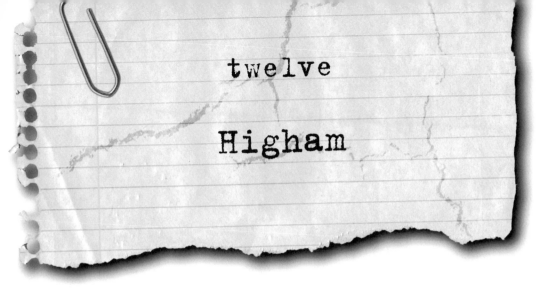

twelve

Higham

The Hermit Inn

In the late 1970s, the old stone public house in Higham generated public interest when it was taken over by Michael Wall (a former engineer) and his wife Christine. Within a couple of weeks of being there, the couple became so terrified that they vowed to leave. They had witnessed a yellow, glowing face appear one night on their bedroom wall, which expanded and distorted before disappearing. It had two dark areas where the eyes should have been. Scared, the couple

The Hermit Inn (now known as Alan's Lodge), Higham, home to an evil entity. (Authors' collection)

moved bedrooms, but within a few days Michael was woken again, this time by a banging noise coming from the corner of the room. Sitting up in bed, Michael saw the same distorted face on the wall above a clothes rail; when it vanished, the clothes rail collapsed to the floor. Michael said nothing to his wife this time for fear of frightening her even more – the fear was already so great that they had resorted to sleeping with the lights on all night. The face appeared again to the couple – only this time it was grey in colour. It rose to the ceiling and disappeared.

Michael contacted the owner of the pub to see if the previous tenants had reported similar problems, but, as far as the latter was aware, no reports of this nature had ever been made before. Michael and his wife insisted that an exorcism be carried out at the pub, and the owner arranged this with a local priest. The strange entity has not been reported since, but we wonder if it will appear again when a new tenant takes over …

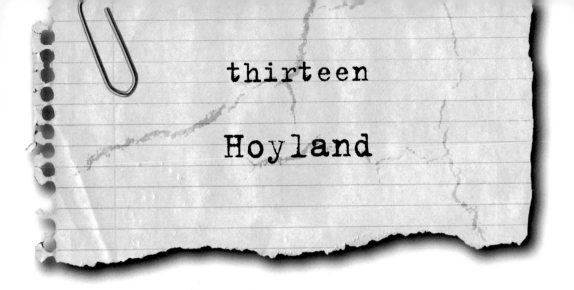

thirteen

Hoyland

Hoyland Lowe Stand

Standing out against the skyline, Hoyland Lowe Stand is situated beside an old graveyard belonging to St Peter's Church. If the building could speak, it would tell fascinating stories of the lives of the rich, of

Hoyland Lowe Stand, showing the window where a figure of a girl has been seen. (Authors' collection)

historical events such as the Civil War, and of many pageants and feasts. Built around 1750, the stand most likely served as a huntsman's lodge and observation point. It later became home for various families connected with the church. There have long been rumours of tunnels running from the tower to a nearby farmhouse and the church; during recent renovation work, the indentation of what appears to be a collapsed tunnel was found, giving credence to the legend. Numerous reports have been made of a little girl dressed in white appearing in the top window of the stand; it is thought that she is the daughter of a family that once lived there. However, our research did not uncover any young deaths related to this building.

St Peter's Church Graveyard

On a dark and cold day in February 2006, at about 6.30 p.m., a local man was walking his dog. The weather was very windy, and, not wanting to be out long, he hurried back through the graveyard past the stand. Suddenly, a white light appeared

St Peter's graveyard, where a figure in white has been seen. (Authors' collection)

before him in the shape of a human figure. He was quite taken aback at the sight and it stopped him dead in his tracks. He stared at the figure for several minutes, before it dispersed just as quickly as it had appeared. At this, he ran out of the graveyard, terribly shaken. He had never believed in such things until that day, and has never again gone there alone after dark.

The Charisma Bar

The building is a former Methodist church built in the early 1800s. During the mid-1990s it was an antiques shop, before being sold and turned into a restaurant in 2003. Today, it is known as the Charisma Bar, named after the previous antiques business.

Leeanne Clegg worked in the restaurant in 2005. One Sunday lunchtime she was cleaning up the third-floor function room after the rush, when she turned around and saw a man standing near the sink in the kitchen. She describes him as wearing a long black coat, holding a prayer book with a red bookmark, and sporting a head of pure white hair, a really big nose and dark eyes. Leeanne said that he reminded her of the vicar in the film *Poltergeist II*. The man walked straight through the sink and wall into the dining room, which used to be a Sunday school hall. Leeanne watched in amazement as he then walked through the tables and chairs towards the stage that used to be the pulpit. He turned around and started preaching to the empty room. After several minutes of this, the man stopped what he was saying, looked up from his book, and stared right at Leeanne in a stern manner before disappearing into thin air. Shocked and shaken, Leeanne fled the building and vowed never to be alone in that room again.

This isn't the only paranormal activity that has been witnessed in the building. Reports were made of cutlery and plates moving from tables in the restaurant and being stacked in their rightful places on shelves. Also, a suit of armour that stood in the grand building for years would often be tampered with, and the sword by its side would be found the following day in a salute position. A well-dressed lady has been seen in the toilet downstairs on the second floor. One unsuspecting person was so frightened at the sight that she came running out in a state of undress. She claimed that she was met by a Grey Lady at the cubicle door, with long white hair and Victorian clothes. Many other people have seen the woman whilst alone in the room. A further incident was reported when two young children were playing around the bar area and were stopped in their tracks by the grey woman, who refused to let them past.

The Charisma – the building when it was in use as the chapel. (Authors' collection)

In 2008 the Charisma suffered damage after a fire broke out around the back of the building. An insurance assessor arrived and took pictures of the rooms to assess the damage for his records. Several days later, he contacted the owner and asked if there were any known hauntings in the building as something unusual had turned up in his photographs. The pictures he had taken showed the figure of a boy in the bar in the function room. It is unknown who the boy is. Many other people have reported the sounds of children singing old hymns, and burnt wood has been smelt on a number of occasions.

It is rumoured that another fire had previously broken out which claimed the lives of the vicar and several children during a Sunday service. However, we have been unable to verify if there was indeed a fire in the old chapel, or if any loss of life resulted from such an incident.

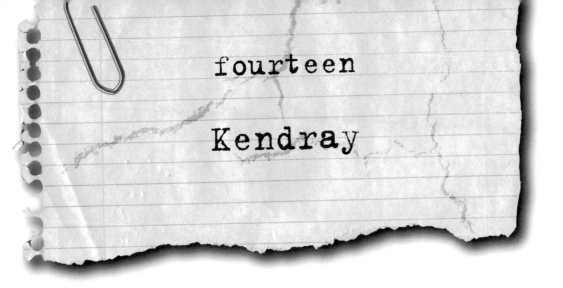

fourteen

Kendray

St Helen's Hospital

St Helen's maternity hospital served Barnsley before Barnsley District General Hospital was built in its place in the 1960s. There have been many reports of ghostly

The Grey Lady in a rocking chair. (Authors' collection)

experiences around the hospital. On the infectious diseases ward – which used to be the children's ward – staff working night shifts have claimed to hear children crying. In addition to this, one of the gynaecology wards, which is now used as office space, is said to be haunted by a young girl called Sally. She could not be resuscitated and staff say that she presses the stomach of anyone who enters the room where she died. Many visitors and staff claim that the ward has an eerie feel. On occasion, shadows have been seen moving around at night, accompanied by unexplained noises. Another ward that is now used as offices is said to be haunted by an old lady with grey hair, who rocks backwards and forwards in her rocking chair before smiling and then just disappearing. Witnesses always say that she appears to be friendly and seems quite content.

The Haunted Terrace

In 1971, a family moved into a house at the top end of Summer Lane, Kendray. The previous owner was named Charlie and had worked all his life down the pits.

After living in the house for around four weeks, one of the children was playing in the back bedroom and happened to look out of the window. He saw a man wearing a flat cloth cap, white shirt, waistcoat, and pit boots, digging at the top of the garden. Thinking that his parents had hired a gardener, he went to see what the man was doing. As the little boy drew closer to the man, he said, 'Hey up.' The man looked up from his digging and said, 'Hey up son.' The boy then asked him his name and was told 'Charlie'. The boy went on to ask, 'What tha doin?' to which Charlie replied, 'Am digging garden, lad.' Charlie then carried on about his business and seemed to be speaking to a third person whom the child couldn't see. All of a sudden Charlie downed his tools and said, 'Am off now love.' He walked down the garden path, down the drive, and out of sight. The little boy went into the house and told his parents about Charlie digging the garden. His parents, knowing that the house had belonged to a man named Charlie, scolded him for telling tales and wanted to know who had given him the information. To this day, the boy – now a grown man – swears blind that he saw Charlie digging in the garden.

Kendray Cottage

The property is nestled away in Kendray and was built in 1740 as a stable block and farrier's accommodation for Park House, which is now under private ownership. The stable block was later extended and turned into two-up two-down dwellings, whilst the horses were relocated to a new block of stables that later became potting sheds.

After moving into the property in the early 1960s, a family of three, consisting of mother, father and young son, were quite content in their small home until they realised that they were sharing it with something else. The man of the house was the first to experience the strange events. One day, he heard screaming coming from downstairs. Thinking that someone was hurt he went to investigate, only to find that the back door was wide open and the noise was coming from the garden. He wandered outside and was shocked to see a man roaming around the garden wearing a three-cornered hat and holding a walking stick. What horrified him most was that the man didn't appear to have any legs – it was as if he was walking through the ground, wading his way through the soil. The stranger never acknowledged him and carried on walking in the darkness of the garden.

Stumbling back into the house where his wife and son stood waiting, the man had to be helped to a chair and given a stiff drink. It was only after two hours that he was finally able to tell them what he had seen. It was then that they realised the ground had been raised and the figure would have been walking on the original cobbled courtyard.

This was just the start of the activity. One day, whilst they were all watching television, the locked door started to bang repeatedly. The television then slowly

Kendry Cottage, which now stands empty, where the figure in a tricorn hat was seen. (Authors' collection)

dragged itself across the room towards the unsuspecting family on the couch. Just as it got to the point where the cables were fully stretched, the banging ceased and the television stopped moving. The family were stricken with fear. More events unfolded, including bedcovers being ripped from them while they were sleeping, and scratching noises under their beds. The man of the house then suffered a stroke and was taken seriously ill. This seemed to escalate the hauntings and he often complained about the bed shaking violently and being lifted off the floor. This was also witnessed by his wife and son on numerous occasions. Taps began to turn themselves on and his wife even

considered calling in a priest to exorcise the house.

Unfortunately, the man passed away and things got so bad that the family decided to leave the house forever. As they were moving, their neighbour enquired about their reasons for departing. After they had explained the events, the neighbour informed them that they had experienced similar things and had often seen the man in the hat wandering around the garden. They believed it to be Jacob Hanshaw, who was trampled to death by a horse when the place was a stable block. Since the family left, no one has ever lived there for longer than a couple of days. Today the property stands empty. Or does it?

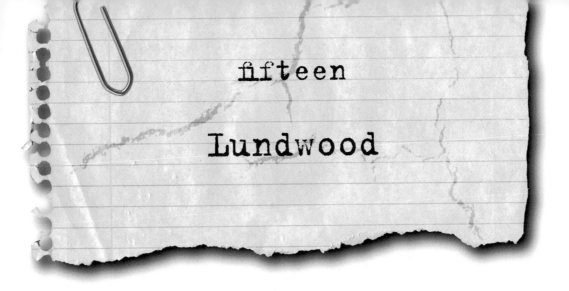

fifteen

Lundwood

Lundwood Isolation Hospital

Lundwood Isolation Hospital, half a mile down Lund Lane, was opened in 1900 to care for smallpox victims. During the First and Second World Wars it was used for victims of shell shock, many of whom sadly contracted illnesses and never left. In 1948 it became a geriatric care hospital, before being demolished in 1977.

For well over thirty years, staff and patients alike reported fleeting dark entities and bizarre occurrences plaguing the hospital. Wheelchairs were seen rolling along the empty corridors late at night, footsteps would keep many a patient awake during hours of darkness, and medical staff wearing old Victorian uniforms were seen. One nurse also claimed to have seen a Grey Lady with a white flowing headdress, resembling that of an early sister's uniform. Sister Rose Webster, who worked at the geriatric hospital, said she often experienced strange events there and her terrier dog steadfastly refused to enter the building. Rose said, 'Even in 1947 most people believed the building was haunted. At least one matron refused to go upstairs. The top floor was really eerie and unnaturally cold.'

The hospital was eventually burned to the ground. A local council officer said that this was a safety precaution, to prevent dormant germ spores being circulated. They dismissed the local rumour that it was burned to purge the place of evil. During the hospital's last days, the Grey Lady was still making her presence felt. Rumour has it that police dogs, on patrol in the grounds since the hospital's closure in September

A photograph of a group of infectious disease nurses from the early 1900s. (Courtesy of Barnsley Reference Library)

Lund Lane – where the hospital once stood. (Authors' collection)

1974, were terrified to enter the building. Although the hospital has long since been reduced to ashes, the ghosts refuse to be laid to rest. During our research for this book, we were approached by a former resident who lived in a property that stood where the old hospital and grounds once were.

In 2004, Jan Harris and her partner moved into the modest bungalow on Lund Lane. Within a week, men turned up to install satellite television. Whilst making the men a cup of tea, Jan overheard them saying, 'I'm fed up of coming here. How long do you think these two will last before the ghosts get 'em?'

Intrigued by their conversation, she asked, 'What's this about ghosts?'

One of the men said, 'Oops, sorry love, I didn't see you there' – but was only too eager to tell her the tale. He said that it was the sixth time within the last four years that they had been called to install a system for a new tenant at this address, but no one had ever stayed long. Every previous tenant had mentioned strange happenings and it had become known to the engineers as the 'haunted bungalow'. They always saw it as an easy job because they didn't have to install a dish, just the receiver. Not taking too much notice of what they had said, she joked about the superstitious engineers later with her partner. However, it wasn't long before the problems started.

A new alarm system, with infrared motion sensors and door contacts, had been installed along with a state-of-the-art control panel that showed where the break was in the system. Soon after this was installed, the alarm started going off for no apparent reason during the early hours of the morning, between 2 and 3 a.m. The control panel showed that the back door had been opened, but, upon checking this, the door was always locked. They would reset the alarm and return to bed, only to be disturbed again by the motion sensor in the lounge. When checking this, they noticed that the lounge door had been opened. This occurrence became so frequent that they had to call the alarm company out on several occasions to check the system for a fault; no fault could ever be found. They even had the lounge door checked by a joiner to make sure it was hung correctly. In the end, they had no option but to disconnect the system altogether.

The back bedroom, at this point, was freezing cold; even with additional heaters in the room, they could never get the temperature to rise. It was so bad that they could see their breath in the air and had to relocate to the front bedroom; even the dog refused to enter the room and would bark

at the doorway as if there was a stranger in there. The phenomena increased and so did the strain on the couple. Things would go missing and only reappear after a small domestic had ensued; it was almost as if the pair were being baited into an argument by the entity. Both of them frequently witnessed fleeting shadows, even though they didn't like to talk about it. Jan said that she often saw a tall figure standing in the lounge doorway, which would vanish when she turned her gaze its way.

With the increase in activity, the dog's behaviour became more erratic; it barked and growled at thin air, becoming more anxious over time, and it wasn't long before it disappeared and was never seen again. Jan's partner remained stoic against the strange phenomena – until one day, when the plug in

A plug, similar to one that was seen spinning. (Authors' collection)

the bathroom sink began to spin wildly even though he hadn't touched it. After this incident he refused to bathe alone and insisted that Jan didn't leave him alone in the room.

One evening, while they were in the lounge watching television, a bright magnolia light manifested next to Jan at about head height; she described it as being about the size of a football, but an oval shape. She shouted to her partner, who was sat in a chair, but he'd already seen it. They stared in disbelief for around thirty seconds before it vanished. Jan recounted the story of the orb to her daughter when she visited later that week. Her daughter wasn't surprised, as she had seen the same light in the back bedroom during a previous visit. The couple knew that they had to leave, in order to avoid the haunting and oppressive atmosphere that was damaging their relationship.

Not long after coming to this decision, a close friend of Jan's came to visit. She pulled into the long driveway and knocked on the front door, but there was no answer because the couple were out shopping. Getting back in her car, the friend began reversing down the drive when she noticed someone at the window. Thinking this was Jan, she stopped – but was horrified to see the incomplete, partly transparent, torso of a woman in some sort of uniform standing at the window and waving slowly from left to right.

After hearing her friend's story, Jan decided that they needed to move out that weekend. A removal company had already taken most of their furniture, and all that was left were a few personal belongings and boxes. But during the final move, Jan refused point blank to enter the house and shouted instructions to her partner to hurry up. In the late afternoon, Jan noticed a bright blue fluorescent glow emitting from the lounge. She shouted to her partner, 'What you messing with the tele for? You know I don't want to be here after dark!' Her partner came back to the door and said, 'Jan, the TV went with the removal men! You're freaking me out now. Come and help me get the last of the stuff so we can get out of here!' But as Jan stepped into the hallway, she could see dozens of shadows encroaching and a feeling of impending doom swept over her. She and her partner dropped the boxes and fled, never returning to pick them up.

Jan often wonders what happened to the haunted bungalow, and if any occupants ever stayed there longer than a few months. After receiving this story we went to look at the location she described, but we think it may now have been demolished, just like the old hospital that stood there before. ...

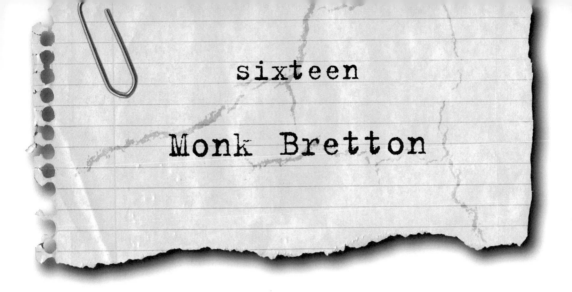

sixteen

Monk Bretton

Monk Bretton has been a settlement since medieval times. The vague shapes of men in long gowns have been seen running around this area, and the sounds of chanting have been heard in the dead of night.

Monk Bretton Priory

Monk Bretton Priory was founded by monks from the Priory of St John at Pontefract in the twelfth century. In the

Monk Bretton Priory – view from inside the old ruin. (Authors' collection)

1680s, local gentry first recorded sightings of a ghostly black friar. A man riding his steed through the priory grounds early one morning had decided to take a look at the magnificent structure. As he got closer, he could see what he thought was a local peasant girl wandering around the grand estate. He rode towards her to bid her good morning, but when he reached the curtain wall it dawned on him that the hooded figure was not a maiden in a shawl but a man in a habit, gliding through the fog in an unearthly manner. The figure turned its head in the direction of the rider, and, before he knew what was happening, it was upon him. Startled, the man gazed down at the hooded figure in awe, only for it to reveal a hideous, skeletal face which struck fear into the core of his soul. At this, the horse reared and bolted, nearly causing the rider to fall off. The horse did not stop until it reached Worsbrough.

Over the years the man recounted the story to family and friends, describing the black friar who resembled the Grim Reaper himself. He believed that the entity had been a warning, and that he would have died if he had continued on his journey that day. The tale has subsequently slipped into local folklore, where it resides today.

An impression of the ghostly Black Friar. (Courtesy of Barnsley Central Library)

The Bailey Club

The Bailey Club in Monk Bretton has always been popular with locals and visitors. Perhaps people are drawn to the mysterious music heard there. The sounds of the hymn 'All People That on Earth do Dwell' is often heard being played on the club's organ, stopping conversations while patrons try to recognise the psalm and look for the source. Many staff and customers have gone to investigate the music. Upon tracing it back to the club's organ, the music abruptly stops and no organist can be found. A ghostly monk has been seen lurking around the Bailey Club and is thought to be the likely culprit for the beautiful melodies. On one occasion, an icy blast of cold cut through the building with such force that patrons thought the doors had burst open through freak weather conditions. They were surprised to find that all openings to the building were secure – which caused a second chill to run down their spines!

seventeen

New Lodge

New Lodge Woods

One winter's night, around 8 p.m., a group of children were in the woods when they heard a sound that was like a train heading towards them. Not thinking much of it, they carried on playing – until about five minutes later, when the group saw a long white shadow which resembled train carriages fly past them. The 'train' took about fifteen seconds to pass, as they stood there frozen with fear. Astounded, the group ran home, shaken and scared at what they had seen.

We have been unable to trace if there were once any train lines in this area.

eighteen

Newmillerdam

Chevet Hall

Chevet Hall, purchased by the Pilkington family in 1765, once stood to the east of Newmillerdam Country Park. Locals were not allowed in the grounds and poachers were severely dealt with. Later, Lionel Pilkington had nine lodges built for his gamekeepers, who were charged with protecting the estate. Two of the lodges stand at the park gates, either side of the dam. In the 1960s, Chevet Hall was demolished, due to mining subsidence.

The ghostly figure of a man has been seen at dusk, lurking in the undergrowth in various parts of the park surrounding the lake. Many locals believe that this is the ghost of a poacher. It has been suggested that the man accidently drowned in the lake; a more sinister theory is that he was murdered and his body was discarded in the dam. Both versions conclude that his body was never recovered. Could his soul be waiting for his remains to be found so he can finally be laid to rest? Others claim that he is one of the gamekeepers, still working his shift and protecting the land and lake from the poachers who once stole from the estate.

Newmillerdam, where ghostly figures are often seen. (Authors' collection)

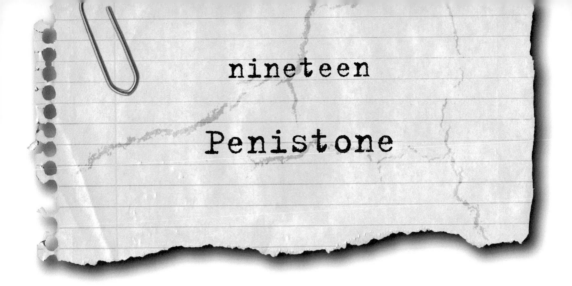

nineteen

Penistone

Cannon Hall

Hidden in the beautiful South Yorkshire village of Cawthorne, just north of Barnsley, is Cannon Hall. Its present owners, Barnsley Council, have opened it as a museum. Part of the estate is still a working farm and this is now a popular visitor attraction. Records show that there was a house on the site as early as 1086; however, not much is written about it. In the late fourteenth century the estate was owned by the Bosville family

Cannon Hall – now a museum. (Authors' collection)

of Ardsley, and it was during this time that the most violent event in the hall's history occurred. The Bosvilles had let the hall to a family whose daughter was romantically linked with a man named Lockwood. Unfortunately, Lockwood had been implicated in the murder of Sir John Eland, the sheriff of the county. The tenant, frightened of being caught harbouring a fugitive, sent word to Bosville, whose men went to Cannon Hall and killed Lockwood in a cruel and violent manner.

In 1660 the estate was bought by John Spencer, who brought his family to Cannon Hall from Montgomeryshire. He hoped that the area was a safer place than Wales for those with Royalist sympathies. The Spencer family continued to use Cannon Hall as their home until the last member of the family, Elizabeth, sold the house to Barnsley Council in 1951.

Cannon Hall has a history of spooky occurrences. The present staff have reported a series of strange events – the majority being experienced in daylight, and some being witnessed by more than one person.

The Entrance Hall

One member of staff, who was working late, was waiting for the last of the visitors to leave when they saw a lady move behind one of the grand columns in the entrance hall. As it was closing time, the staff member followed the woman upstairs to remind her that they were locking up. When the staff member reached the top of the stairs they were greeted by a colleague, who informed them that no one was upstairs and hadn't been for a long time. Thinking that they had imagined the lady, the employee thought no more of it until, whilst leaving, they spotted the same lady on the hall's driveway. After looking at old photographs, they became convinced that the lady they saw twice in one night was Elizabeth Spencer-Stanhope, the last of the family to own Cannon Hall.

The Victorian Ballroom

One member of staff claims that she felt someone tugging at her cheek in this room. Turning around to see who was there, she was spooked to find that she was alone. Later that day, she experienced a resistance to the double door whilst she was unlocking it. She described the incident as if someone was pulling at the door from the other side.

The South Terrace

During the summer of 2005, staff were showing a family around the dining room when the South Terrace door slammed shut for no obvious reason. There was no wind at the time and no explanation could be given for such a violent bang. On another occasion, one of the attendants was opening the door – which normally would open easily – only to find that it wouldn't move more than a few inches. When it suddenly yielded and opened, the room was empty. Another time when the attendant was locking this door, the second door shut behind her; she was then 'trapped' between the two doors. She pushed it open in a panic and fled, refusing to lock those doors by herself ever again.

More strange activity was witnessed by staff on 30 August 2007. They watched in amazement as the crystal chandelier in the dining room started to move as if it was a single entity, despite the fact that it consisted of hundreds of separate elements which usually rattle and move independently of each other when touched. The chandelier rotated slowly in a clockwise direction, silently and for four hours without stopping. What was particularly strange about this occurrence was that the supporting chain did not move or rotate. The staff investigated possible causes for this throughout the incident, and when it stopped they tried to recreate the phenomenon by moving the chandelier, but they couldn't achieve the same effect. No possible cause has been found for this to date.

The Library

Freshly smoked pipe tobacco is often smelt by visitors and staff alike. One member of staff reported feeling her hair being stroked when she was on duty in the room, leaving her unnerved and shaken.

The Kitchen

The figure of a young woman dressed in a maid's uniform has been seen by several staff in the kitchen; others also report the feeling of being watched when they are alone in the room. Other strange phenomena have included a coffee machine turning itself on, a door unlocking itself, a poker from the fire range flying across the room and hitting a member of staff on the leg, and a stoneware jar suddenly 'flying' from a shelf and smashing on the floor.

The Upstairs Corridor

Muffled voices can often be heard along the corridor, as well as furniture being moved around in the end room. This leaves staff baffled as the room is always locked and not accessible to the public. A visitor once reported seeing a 'hazy figure'; she reported this to staff, who realised that it matched a previous report of a strange woman seen in the hall. This woman had seemed so real that the member of staff had started a conversation with her, only to discover that she was talking to thin air.

The Green Bedroom

One of the bedrooms in the house is known as the Green Bedroom. This is said to be haunted by a lady who died there during childbirth. A museum attendant claims to have seen the figure of a small woman with long dark hair, wearing a long dark dress, glide into the Green Bedroom one night. Upon checking that the room was empty, the staff member could not explain where she had come from or where she had gone.

The Spencer Room

The Spencer Room is situated above the old stables and is now used for meetings. In October 2006, two female volunteers, who were helping out with an event there, were startled to see a metal teaspoon levitate from out of a cup and land some distance away on the counter. Both ladies said that it was as if the spoon was being lifted out by hand – but they couldn't see the hand!

The Craft Shop

At the museum is a shop named Butlers Pantry, and even here paranormal occurrences have been reported. Toys are said to move by themselves in front of staff and customers. And just outside the shop is a disabled toilet which is known to flush itself just after the lights suddenly go out for no reason. No cause for this has been found to date, despite investigation by electricians and plumbers.

The Deer Shed

The most well-known ghost associated with the hall isn't seen in the hall itself, but has been witnessed in the park at the deer shed. Apparently, in late Victorian times the ghostly image of a tall figure dressed in a long coat was seen materialising under a tree near the shed. Accounts show that in 1881 the vicar of Cawthorne, Revd Charles Tiplady Pratt, conducted an exorcism near the deer shed. This was regarded as successful, as there were no further sightings. Or were there?

Catling Hall

Catling Hall was built in the sixteenth century, taking its name from the family who resided there. When Frank Henry Gaunt took over the hall, he frequently laid down food to encourage the foxes for the local hunts. Donald Nutbrown, a young lad, would visit the hall and help Mr Gaunt in his work. One day, they were outside the hall when a tall gentleman in Edwardian dress appeared from the direction of Gunthwaite Hall and walked past them both, in the direction of Penistone. He offered no greeting to the pair and appeared not to have noticed them. Donald was curious about the strange man's clothing and asked Mr Gaunt who he was. Mr Gaunt replied, 'The figure only appears at certain times of the year and he walks the same route.' He went on to explain that he was not a living person, but in fact a ghost! Mr Gaunt had seen the smartly dressed spectre a number of times and didn't fear the unknown man. He told Donald that, at one time, the old footpath that ran past the hall was used in the transportation of convicts going from Halifax Gaol to the gaol at Sheffield. Catling Hall was a stop-off point for the guards and prisoners to rest; at the time, it was equipped with secure holding places for the criminals.

An illustration of the old chain-gangs, showing the conditions they were subjected to.
(Courtesy of Barnsley Reference Library)

Conditions for transporting prisoners were notoriously bad, and it is likely that many died on the long, treacherous journey. Gaunt informed Donald that, at certain times of the year, he had heard the sounds of rattling chains and eerie groans carried on the wind over the moors.

Dog and Partridge

The Dog and Partridge public house was once used to store dead bodies which were found on the nearby moorland. It is believed that a few of these unfortunates have remained earthbound, and are now seen as fleeting shadows from the corner of one's eye. Strange smells have also been reported coming from the cellars below.

St John's Church

One warm summer's evening in July 1793, the newly ordained curate of St John's Church, Thomas Hunter, stood at dusk in the churchyard watching the birds roosting in the trees. Darkness was just falling when his eyes were drawn to a pale blue light hovering over a certain spot in the churchyard. Thinking it was a lantern, and fearing grave robbers, he opened the gate to check. However, the light remained fixed for some time, swaying around an old grave. The minister observed it for a while as it began to grow in size and brightness, pulsating like the beating of a heart. Then, little by little, the light began to move slowly, drifting in and out of the gravestones; he cautiously went forward and marked the place where the blue light had first appeared with a stone. He followed it across the road and into the wood; his heart was racing but his curiosity was too strong not to investigate.

The light was moving fast now and building up speed; he had to move at a good pace to keep up with it. When it came out of the wood onto a stretch of open moor, the minister found himself running after it. Finally, it slowed down as he approached some buildings and it came to rest on the door of a farmhouse. As he looked on in amazement, a second, smaller, orb of blue light appeared at an upstairs window, and after some moments of wavering it came through the glass, moving down to align itself on the door next to the first light. Slowly at first, then more briskly, the two began the return journey to the churchyard, with the larger light leading the way. Thomas was almost out of breath when the twin lights reached the churchyard. Entering through the gate a second time, he saw them merging together and fading. He arrived at the scene just in time to mark the spot with another stone.

The next morning the minister returned to the churchyard and found the marker stones; they were at either end of the same horizontal gravestone. Thomas made a mental note of the position of the grave and the name engraved upon it. He then checked the registers, as there didn't seem to have been anyone buried in the family plot for some time. After finding the listing, he learned that no one had been buried there for the last nineteen years.

An artist's impression of what was seen that night. (Courtesy of Barnsley Reference Library)

Thinking that the lights must have been his imagination, he thought nothing more of it until the following day, when he saw the senior deacon talking to the sexton in the churchyard. As he joined them he knew immediately that they were standing near the spot he had identified the previous night. As he came closer, he could see that the sexton was opening up the grave. Making enquiries, Thomas was informed that a boy had died of scarlet fever the previous night. The unfortunate youngster had been the only child in the third generation of a family who lived above the wood in a remote farmhouse. The physician had been hopeful that the boy would recover, but a sudden and unexpected relapse had proved him wrong. The child had died, surrounded by his distraught family, at sunset.

Such lights are often described as corpse candles. For centuries it was believed that life was represented by light, and when death occurred the soul would leave the body in the form of a flame. The lights supposedly serve as an omen of impending death, appearing at the house of a person near death and then making their way to the churchyard by the same route that the coffin would follow. The two lights in the story are different sizes, clearly representing the youngster and his older relative. Similarly, people who have had near-death experiences sometimes report being met by a loved one, who has come to take them to the other side.

The Penistone Ghost Bus

Tales of the Penistone ghost bus have been passed down through several generations around Barnsley. However, the ghost bus is not a new phenomenon but the reincar-

An impression of the ghostly death bus. (Authors' collection)

nation of a much older legend – the death coach, or ghost carriage. These tales date back to medieval times, when it was believed that Death travelled by a pitch black horse-drawn coach. Once the coach has come to earth, it can never return empty. With each passing century it seems that Death finds a more familiar mode of transport to help trick unsuspecting passengers. It is believed that he takes the form of a human and searches for people who are restless or ungrateful with their gift of life, choosing them as his victims on a route direct to hell. The vehicle may change but its purpose is always the same. It appears in many forms, such as a horse-drawn stagecoach, a steam train, a ship like the *Flying Dutchman*, condemned to eternally sail the seas – or a bus, as in the Penistone ghost bus.

The bus arrives late at night to pick up its passengers who are running late. It is reported to be a very old vehicle, in need of repairs, that you board at the rear. The conductor, who is a small, frail old man, always welcomes the passenger on and informs them that the ride is free. Only then, when the bus begins its journey, can the victim see the true form of the passengers and the driver – who are all already dead!

The legend that circulates Barnsley is as follows: Late one night in Penistone, a young man went to catch the last bus home to Barnsley after staying longer than expected talking to his friend. As he could see no one standing at the stop on Barnsley Road, he thought that he had missed the bus. He was about to turn back when he was met by an old man who had come to wait at the same stop. The man said, in an Irish accent, 'You've not missed it son, it'll be along in a minute.' Feeling reassured, the young man hung around waiting for the bus to arrive, exchanging small talk with the old man.

As if out of nowhere, a dimly lit old bus pulled up. The man could see through the dirty windows that there were a few old people on board. He thought it was strange that he had to board at the back of the bus as opposed to the front. However, he ignored the odd-ities because he was glad to be going home. Climbing aboard, he was met by a thin, gaunt-looking ticket conductor, who gestured to the empty seats, saying, 'Jump on. I almost missed you two.'

The young man proceeded to one of the empty seats, closely followed by the Irishman. He noticed that all the other pas-sengers were silent and dressed in black. Before he could take another step, the Irishman abruptly grabbed his left arm, stopping him in his tracks, whilst at the same time pointing at one of the old passengers on the bus, shouting, 'I know you!' Then the Irishman began to pull on the young man's clothes, saying, 'Get off this bus, it's not for us, it's not our bus. GET OFF NOW!' The young man, who was confused and surprised at the strength of the old Irishman's grip, did as he was told. They both stumbled back off the bus onto the pavement, and the old man let go of his arm as they stood watching the bus leave. The young man demanded an explanation.

'Young man, you are lucky coming across me tonight otherwise you would have been in deadly trouble.'

Seeing the fear in the old man's eyes, the lad asked, 'Why?'

'Has no one ever told you to avoid the old bus late at night?'

The authors' impression of the bus driver. (Author's collection)

'What the hell are you going on about?' snapped the young man.

The Irishman took a deep breath, as if to summon up the last dregs of courage, and said, 'I recognised that old man at the front of the bus; he was an old acquaintance of mine and not a very nice man at that.'

'So what's that got to do with getting off the bloody bus?' said the young man, by now quite annoyed.

The old man answered slowly. 'The reason I'm late for the last bus is … is…' He paused for a moment before fixing his gaze firmly on the young man's eyes. 'I've just come back from his wake! He is surely already on the way to the land of the dead, and I for one had no intention of joining him, for I'm sure that was the death bus used by the Grim Reaper himself to harvest the souls of the damned.'

The following account was submitted to us: Two girls had been studying late at college on a cold and windy Friday night. At about 11 p.m. they left to catch a bus back to Penistone. As they chatted and waited at the bus stop, they became a little jumpy because the road was dark and isolated. They were beginning to think they'd missed the last bus, when a rickety old bus appeared from the shadows; it was an old-fashioned sort, where you board at the rear and pay a conductor. When they boarded, they noticed that it was empty apart from the creepy-looking conductor, who sported a head of black hair.

After paying the fare, they sat down in the middle of the bus and continued chatting. A short while later their conversation stopped abruptly, as an ice-cold chill swept around them. Both girls looked around, thinking that a window must be open – but they soon forgot about the chill when they saw five really pale people dressed in black sitting behind them. They all had sunken eyes and purple lips, like the blood had been drained from them. But what was worse was their hollow, wide-eyed, trance-like stare. Scared and upset by the morbid scene, they pressed the bell repeatedly for the bus to stop; all the time they were trans-fixed by the deathly looking passengers who were staring motionlessly at them. After what seemed like an eternity, the bus finally came to a stuttering halt. The two girls jumped off the bus, which set off again as soon as their feet hit the floor. Both girls were shaken and scared at what they had seen, and just stared at the bus as it disap-peared round the bend.

They still don't know quite what they saw that night, but both claim they were nearly the next victims of the ghost bus. While being interviewed, one of the girls stated:

> Ghosts have always fascinated me but I always felt that, like most people, I needed to either see it, or feel it, to believe it. This story is all too real for me, because I was there and saw it with my own eyes. I don't know to this day why we experienced what we did that night, but I know what I saw and nobody will ever convince me that it was not the ghost bus, because I was not alone or the only one to see it!

Ghostly Passengers

It's not just the ghost bus that haunts the roads from Penistone to Barnsley – there are also ghostly passengers. Several drivers have reported running an empty bus back to the depot, only for the bell to ring as if a pas-senger wants to disembark. The orange stop light on the dashboard is on, but when they look through the passenger mirror, there is no one there! Drivers have even stopped the bus to search for their forgotten passen-ger, but have found no soul aboard.

One night, a driver was returning to the bus depot with the internal lights out. He had checked that the bus was empty before setting off. As he went past Noblethorpe Park, he glanced in the passenger mirror and was startled to see a large black figure in the seat next to the luggage rack. He swerved in shock but quickly regained control and pulled the bus over. He switched the lights on to get a better look but the figure had gone. Scared, the driver decided to leave the internal lights on for the rest of his journey. Before he had gone more than 500 yards, he saw the dark figure in the corner of his eye standing next to him, as if wanting to get off at the next stop. The driver stopped the bus right there, but the mysterious figure once again eluded him. He got out of his seat and frantically searched the bus, to no avail. We wonder if the ghostly passengers, just like the two girls who gave us their account, simply caught the wrong bus!

Cubley Hall

Cubley Hall was initially a farm and coun-try residence, then an orphanage, and is now a hotel. The hall has a resident ghost who is thought to be Florence Loxley, who married there in the early 1900s. Guests over the years have reported seeing a woman dressed in a long, blue, flowing gown standing over beds and staring at the person sleeping there. It is only when the person wakes that she disappears.

A similar account comes from a lady who stayed there as a child. One bonfire night she went to bed poorly and, on waking, she saw a lady in a long gown standing at the

An artist's impression of the ghost seen frequently by guests. (Courtesy of Barnsley Reference Library)

bottom of her bed. The lady was smiling at her in a caring fashion. The young girl was startled for a moment but then screamed and the ghost left.

Many newlyweds have reported being greeted in an approving manner by the ghost of Flo as they descend the staircase to breakfast; this is considered to be a good omen for a happy marriage. Passers-by have also seen Flo standing in the window when the building wasn't in use.

Old Hanna Lane

Old Hanna Lane runs from Penistone Grammar School to Work Bank Lane. A lady wearing 1960s clothing has been seen here on numerous occasions.

One evening, a group of girls decided to park their cars on the lane to have a cigarette. As one of them started her car to go home, she looked up and was surprised to see a woman standing before her dressed in '60s clothing with a small white dog. The woman walked around to the driver's window before vanishing into thin air.

Another incident took place when two boys were out riding bikes along the same road. One of the boys rode off in front and went around the bend, where he came face to face with a woman dressed in a long flowery dress, and a '60s-style coat and hat, walking her dog. The boy stopped and shouted to his friend, 'Watch out! There's someone in the road!' But his friend came round the corner and laughed, saying, 'What you on about? There's no one there.' And to his surprise the woman had vanished, along with her dog. The boys looked across the fields surrounding them, but she was nowhere to be seen.

Many of the locals seem to think that it's Hanna herself walking the road, but during our research we were unable to trace why the street has become known as Old Hanna Lane!

The Haunted Farm

Out in the open fields near Penistone is an old abandoned farm. No one has lived there for over 100 years; it has stood derelict following rumours of a haunting. Most families who moved in didn't stay for long. The ghost is said to be one of the previous owners, who parades the kitchen during the small hours of the morning, banging and crashing around in search of something. The last known owner was driven to such desperation that he offered a handsome reward to anyone who would sit up for a night and confront the apparition.

A local from a nearby village volunteered himself and a farm boy to undertake the task. They shut themselves into the haunted kitchen and, at midnight, as they were seated by the fire, they felt a cold wind blow round them. Turning suddenly, they saw the figure of an old man standing behind them. They froze with fear but, not wanting to flee and lose the promised reward, they asked the ghost its reason for haunting the farm; the ghostly old man said nothing but pointed to the hearthstone in the kitchen. He beckoned them to remove it.

As soon as daylight broke, the man and boy set about lifting the heavy hearthstone. To their great surprise, they found a large bag of money concealed beneath it, which was divided between them as a reward for their courage. However, the noises continued and the farmer decided to leave the farm as many had done before him. The farm had acquired such a reputation that no one ever took it on again. So, the old farm sits alone on the hillside undisturbed, waiting for the next tenant.

A recreation of a grave-robbing. (Courtesy of Barnsley Reference Library)

The Old Crown Inn

The Old Crown Inn was once associated with resurrection men. During the early years of the nineteenth century, the demand for corpses for dissection by medical students reached its peak. The value of corpses was high, and fresh graves were closely guarded by family members. The trade was so profitable that people were prepared to take risks and would enter the graveyards late at night to dig up newly buried corpses. In Yorkshire the problem wasn't as bad as it was in other areas, but nevertheless many graves were robbed. The best markets for fresh cadavers could be as far away as Durham and York. This meant it sometimes took several days to negotiate the terms of sale and delivery.

A cold store was sometimes required for the corpses, and a pub cellar was considered to be ideal. The authorities had strong suspicions about Penistone's Old Crown Inn and what lay beneath the feet of unsuspecting drinkers. Formal investigations began after a watch was sold on the premises that had belonged to a recently buried body. However, there was no firm evidence that the watch had been sold there and it was never retrieved, therefore no criminal charges were brought.

Reports have been made from residents living near the churchyard that the sound of digging can be heard in the dead of night; also, the sound of a distressed wailing woman has been heard coming from one of the graves.

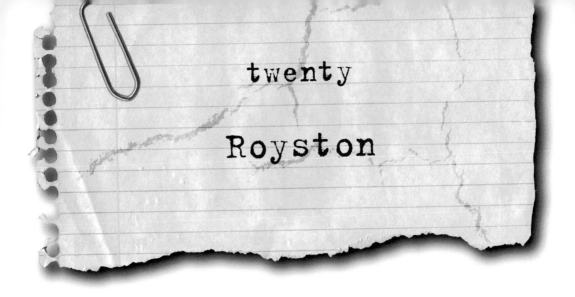

twenty

Royston

The Royston Ghost

On a cold winter's night, the 12b train was travelling from Monkton to Royston, bringing workers home from the coking factory. A thick fog had swept in from the coast, masking the moon and leaving the line and track in darkness. As the train approached a tunnel, the driver was surprised to see an old man dressed in a trench coat slowly tottering across the tracks. The driver applied the brakes immediately, but it was too late and the train struck him.

The train driver was very distressed and stopped the train. He got out to look for the old man but couldn't find any trace of him, or any sign that the train had hit anyone. Confused, he climbed back in, started the engine and continued his journey. But just before the train arrived at Royston, an apparition of the old man appeared in front of him and whispered, 'Sleep safely this night, as it will be your last. …' All the passengers on the train died mysteriously that night, and the line was closed.

After looking into this story, we were informed that 12b wasn't a train number that ever ran on the Royston main line –

trains had a seven digit number back then. Secondly, although there was and still is a coke works at Monkton, it's only a two-minute walk away from the former Royston railway station site, so there would be no need to catch a train home. Not that workers could anyway – Monkton never had a railway station! Also, there is no tunnel anywhere on the Royston line. The tracks are still used to this day (for freight only) and have never closed. We have to conclude that this Royston ghost is an urban legend.

An illustration of the ghost train, which is supposed to run through Royston. (Courtesy of Barnsley Reference Library)

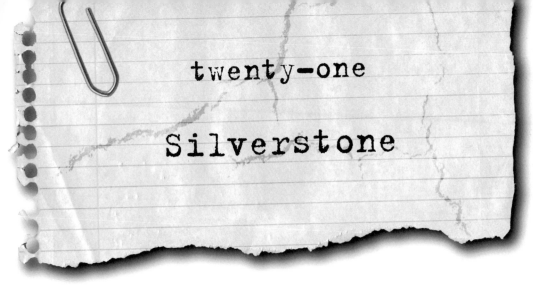

twenty-one

Silverstone

Silverstone Scout Camp

Silverstone Scout Camp is in the foot-hills of the Pennines, between the picturesque villages of Silkstone and Dodworth. Silverstone was used as an army training camp during the First World War, then was gifted to local Scout groups. The site is now run by a group of Scout volunteers and is one of the most successful Scout camps in the UK. One Scout leader took a group of boys to the camp in the summer of 1985 – and got more than he bargained for. The following story was provided to us by Andy Beecroft, from Hull.

The summer camp was always held during the first week of the summer holidays at the end of July. On the night in question, one of the Scout leaders went to the pub at the bottom of the hill and said that he would return at about 10.30. The task of checking the tents was left to Andrew Beecroft, who was there with his pregnant wife and four-year-old son. Andrew left his wife and son in the tent and looked over the views while waiting for his friend to return. At about 10.30, the light summer sky was illuminating the site a

little. Andrew saw a figure coming towards him across the field and presumed it was his friend returning from the pub. However, this figure seemed to be dressed in a dark uniform. Andrew called over to him but received no response. The figure carried on walking towards Andrew until it was barely a metre away from him, then it turned approximately 180° very sharply. Andrew followed him, annoyed that the man hadn't acknowledged him, and tried to tap him on the shoulder … at which point the man just vanished. A couple of seconds later, it dawned on Andrew what had happened – he'd seen a ghost! He rushed back to the tent to tell his wife, who, in her state, just didn't want to know. Ten minutes later, his friend returned from the pub.

The next morning, the part-time camp warden visited Andrew, like he did most mornings. Andrew told him what he'd seen, and the warden casually said, 'You've only seen the old railway guard – loads of people have seen him!' The railway guard had lived in the village and was dropped off each night at the back of the campsite. One evening, he'd gone home a different way than normal, and had accidentally fallen down one of the opencast mine workings that had existed in the woods many years ago. He had died of exposure before he was found the next day.

In addition to this ghost, rumour has it that the area was, at one time, a Viking settlement, and people have reported seeing Viking feasts taking place in the woods. Thinking at first that the revellers are Scouts, witnesses are shocked when the sight before them disappears.

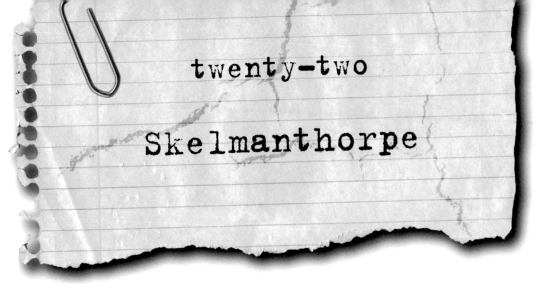

twenty-two

Skelmanthorpe

Cruck Barn

At the top of Lodge Street in Skelmanthorpe is a listed building that started life a cruck barn. To the rear of the building is a door with a love heart, on which the names William and Mary Oxley are carved. A marriage between a William Oxley and a Mary Wainwright is recorded in the local parish registers of 1688.

Today, there are often reports of the smell of burning wood, followed by the image of a woman appearing out of a black mist. Could this be the ghost of Mary Wainwright, who was tragically killed in a fire at the barn?

An illustration of Mary's faithful death. (Authors' collection)

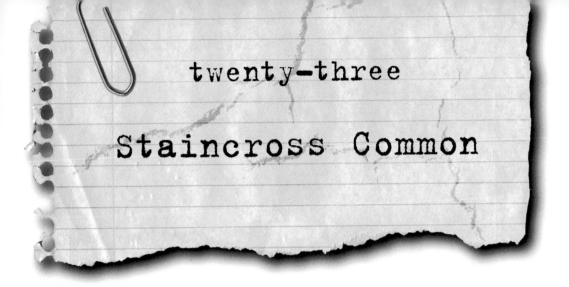

twenty-three

Staincross Common

Wheatley Woods

Wheatley Woods is on the outskirts of Staincross Common, between Woolley village and Warren Lane. Many locals have felt uneasy when visiting the woods, and it is rare to find anyone brave enough to explore the area after dark. However, one night a group of friends decided to go there to investigate the legend. Setting off from Woolley, the group of four were quite unafraid as they felt there was safety in numbers. As they approached the woods through the fields, they heard the sound of a drum beating. It was dark and no light could be seen, but as they got closer to the woods the drumming got louder. A little scared at first, they just stood and listened. The sound didn't stop. After listening for several minutes, the group plucked up the courage to investigate.

They entered the woodland along the footpath, and the noise seemed to be coming from all around them: no one spot could be identified as the source. Then one of them looked back from where they had walked and shouted, 'Look at that!' The group looked around and saw a tall shaft of light emanating from the ground, right at the opening of the woods. It was about the width of an average person and roughly 6ft high. Bizarrely, the glow didn't seem to light anything around it. The drumming noise continued as the group looked on in fright. Then, all of a sudden, the light went out and the drumming stopped, leaving the woods in an eerie, silent darkness.

During our research, we were told by locals that there used to be a mine shaft at the entrance of the woods. A miner hadn't returned home one evening so his wife had gone to look for him. Whilst out searching, she had slipped into the shaft and died before she was found. Could her spirit be responsible for the light? There is also a rumour that the mine shafts were used by Cavaliers during the English Civil War, to enable them to move around during the day without being discovered by the patrolling Roundheads. They used the beat of a drum to guide them through the tunnels in the darkness.

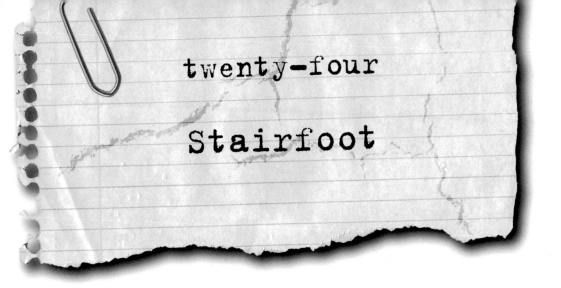

twenty-four

Stairfoot

Victoria Street

Nestled away in the side streets of Stairfoot is a road named Victoria Street. It looks like any other street in the area, but, behind the stone-clad walls, a haunting took place that left a whole family in fear. They have been unable to talk about their experiences until now, over twenty years later.

In 1974, the Tudor family moved in with their eight-month-old daughter. Several years went by and the small family grew as the couple had a further two children – a girl, then later a boy. It wasn't until 22 December 1989 that things changed for the family forever. Like most, the family were looking forward to Christmas, and were discussing the various events they had planned over the Christmas period. Dad was at work at the time, and Mum was in the lounge with her youngest daughter; her son was lying on the sofa listening to the radio. All of a sudden, Mrs Tudor stopped in mid-conversation as the jet black figure of a man, hunched over on all fours, with his back arched like a startled cat, scurried across the living room floor like a frantic arachnid. Wide-eyed in disbelief, she said to her daughter, 'Did you

see that?' The daughter had. Both speechless, they waited for the figure to emerge from behind the chair where they assumed it was hiding; they could hear the sound of a scratching noise like a crisp bag being crumpled, or the crackling of static electricity. After a few minutes of waiting, Mrs Tudor stood up and cautiously moved over to the chair. She peered over but, to her amazement, there was nothing there.

The family discussed what had happened with Mr Tudor the following morning, but he didn't believe their story and said it was their overactive imaginations. The adults agreed not to dwell on it too much as they didn't want to upset the children.

But things went a step further that night while Mr Tudor was working a night shift. Mrs Tudor was woken by her son, who crawled into her bed. This was something he'd done many times before, but perhaps the events of the previous day had caused this particular midnight move. Knowing that her son wriggled around in his sleep, Mrs Tudor got into his bed, which was the bottom bunk in the next room. She lay there for a while before falling asleep, and then was awoken by loud banging and rattling noises coming from upstairs – like all Bedlam had been let loose!

Thinking it was her two daughters, she waited for the noises to cease, but they continued and were getting worse. It was only when her youngest daughter climbed out of the bunk above that she realised her oldest daughter was in the attic alone. Mrs Tudor got up immediately and headed for the attic. As she opened the door, she was met by her oldest daughter running down the stairs and straight past her into the corridor, shouting, 'Mam! Mam! Shut the door! There's summat up there!' Mrs Tudor could clearly see that her daughter was petrified, and slammed the door shut. The noises stopped as quickly as they had started. She then turned to her daughter and said, 'What were you doing up there?' but her daughter explained that the noises hadn't been made by her. There was something else in the attic, something that she couldn't see, and it was dragging the furniture across her room and slamming it into her bed! Drawers were opening and closing on their own, and toys had been flung through the air inches from her face while she'd lain in the darkness too afraid to even move. The pair didn't sleep that night and Mrs Tudor knew that she needed help; particularly now that the entity had attacked her family. Again she mentioned the night's activities to her husband, but again he dismissed her claims.

On Christmas Eve, Mrs Tudor went to see the local vicar, Mr Evans from Ardsley Church. He decided to go straight round to the property and perform a blessing. Upon arriving at the house, Mr Evans went up to the attic and said a prayer, whilst sprinkling holy water around the room. 'For if God spared not the angels that sinned, but cast them down to hell and delivered them into chains of darkness to be reserved unto judgement.'

He finished his prayers and commanded the entity to leave. The temperature in the room seemed to increase and Mr Evans said that everything should now be alright. He then bid the family a good night and left. The family felt at ease and settled down to enjoy the rest of their Christmas undisturbed.

Christmas Day arrived and the extended family came to spend the day with the Tudors. The day was fun and everyone was having a good time. However, Mrs Tudor's eldest daughter was tired and decided to go up to her room in the attic for a while to get away from her noisy family. Running up the two flights of stairs, she burst open her bedroom door – to be confronted by a man who was sat on her bed, wearing a black trilby and cloak. He was just sitting there, silent and motionless, with his head in his hands. The girl was petrified and screamed at the top of her lungs as she ran back down the stairs, through the kitchen, and out into the backyard. Mrs Tudor ran after her daughter and asked why she was screaming. It took the girl a while to come round, but finally she told her mum what she had seen in her room.

Mrs Tudor then asked the girl's father to go upstairs with her and check out the claims – but the room was empty, with not even an imprint on the bed where the man had sat. Mrs Tudor declared that enough was enough and set off to get Mr Evans. But upon arriving at the vicar's home, it soon became apparent that he wasn't there – he was spending Christmas with his daughter and wouldn't be back for a few days. Now at her wits' end, she frantically went on the search for another vicar. Finally, she found a vicar at St George's Church in Barnsley, but, after explaining the dilemma and the events that had unfolded over the past few days, she was told to go home and deal with it. Feeling completely deflated, she headed off home and nailed the attic door shut. The family spent the night fearfully sleeping in the same room.

Things seemed to calm down a bit after that event, but every so often there were strange occurrences – doors would open on their own (particularly when the Tudors' eldest daughter would walk towards it) and one of the controls on the oven would turn itself on – the family had to stick it down with tape. Mrs Tudor would frequently see orbs in the bedroom, and her husband was now seeing them too. Often the hairdryer would switch on by itself, and the video recorder would vibrate and move across the television, even though it was turned off.

One day, Mrs Tudor went to get the iron from the top of the cellar stairs where it was kept, but, when she opened the door, the iron levitated out of its holder and flew out of the cupboard. She raised her hand to shield her face – had she not, it would surely have hit her. Often, when members of the family opened the kitchen cupboards, items would fly out at speed before crashing to the floor. Mrs Tudor was also physically harmed and would repeatedly feel something nipping at her arm, only to discover bruising where the unseen hands had been.

One evening, whilst in the bath relaxing, a very oppressive feeling came over Mrs Tudor – a feeling of being watched. It was as if there was an entity peering down at her from the ceiling. These feelings were so strong that she jumped out of the bath and ran from the room.

She wasn't the only one to experience something in the bathroom. Her husband was in the shower one night, closing his eyes to wash his hair, when he sensed that someone was in the room with him. Quickly washing the soap from his face, he opened his eyes and discovered that the shower curtain had been pulled right back to the wall, even though the bathroom door was bolted shut.

In 1990, the Tudors had another daughter. On one occasion, Mrs Tudor left her two-week-old baby at the head of her bed, secured between two pillows, while she went to get a bottle. Her blood ran cold in horror when she returned and discovered that her baby had been moved. She had been lifted from the pillows and now lay horizontally across the bottom of the bed; this incident had taken no more than a minute.

Around 1992 the youngest daughter wasn't well and Mr Tudor was looking after her whilst Mrs Tudor went out for the evening. On her return Mrs Tudor was met by her husband, who was clearly shaken; he claimed that whilst his daughter was sleeping on the sofa, an unknown force had lifted her up about 3ft into the air. Jumping out of his chair, he had gently pushed her back down onto the cushions; the child had stayed asleep throughout the whole ordeal. Whatever was haunting the house seemed to affect everyone living there. When their youngest child reached the age of two, and was just learning to talk, she would often look into the corners of the room and say, 'Look Mummy grrrrrr' – which meant monsters. However, when Mrs Tudor looked, there was never anything to be seen.

One Sunday morning, when her son went up to the bathroom, he passed his mum's bedroom door and saw a woman looking out of the window. This scared him into such a state that he ran into the bathroom and locked the door, shouting for someone to come and get him. His mother, who was busy with the Sunday dinner at the time, was reluctant to leave the kitchen. Only when she finally went upstairs to see him did she realise her son's true state of panic as he explained what he had seen.

For Christmas 1993, the little girl of the house received a Little Tikes toy kitchen. The kids had gone to bed after a busy Christmas Day and their father was lying on the sofa relaxing. All of a sudden, unseen hands started to tidy the plastic pots and pans away. Mr Tudor hurriedly woke his wife to tell her what he had seen.

Neighbours would often bang on the wall of the Tudors' house complaining about noise, even though there wasn't anyone in at the time, let alone anyone making any noise. But even when the family was at home, they often heard loud footsteps going up and down the stairs. After investigation, no one could ever be found.

One evening, one of the girls had a friend stay over; however, the friend got more than she bargained for when she realised that someone was staying in the room with them. Thinking it was a relative, the girl had a full conversation with an elderly gentleman. It was only when she was asked who she was talking to that the girl realised he was a ghost!

On New Year's Day 1995, the family were enjoying the festivities and celebrating New Year. There were around twelve family members in the lounge, including Mrs Tudor's brother-in-law, who was sat on the sofa next to her son. At around 5 p.m., all of a sudden the brother-in-law felt an ice-cold blast around the back of his neck; this was followed by what he described as a ball of mist swirling around in front of him. Both he and Mrs Tudor's son saw this. Then he felt the sensation that something or someone had entered his body, and experienced overwhelming feelings of anger, hatred and fear. As he looked down at his arms, he noticed that they no longer looked like his own – they were old and withered. Jumping up, he said to his wife, 'We need to go, NOW!' Then he blacked out, and has no recollection of what unfolded next.

Family members watched as the entity violated his body and took control. He started to rant in an abusive manner at everyone. This was so out of character for the normally placid man that at first they were stunned and thought he was messing about. Then, before they knew what was happening, he darted out of the room and into the kitchen, hurling abuse and making threats. He then picked up a chair from the table and hurled it across the room at a family member – but it seemed to strike an invisible force field and ricocheted to the floor. The family tried to restrain him, but he was too strong. He tried to regain control of himself and fled into the street, jumping into his car that was parked a little way up from the house. He tried desperately to start the car but it failed, so he leapt out – and something seemed to fall out of him. Then he ran down a neighbour's path to take refuge behind a wall. By this time he had started to come round; he could hear the neighbours shouting in the street, 'What the hell is that?' All he could remember afterwards was the sound of scraping claws clambering around on the concrete slabs that lined the pavements. It sounded like a dog running on a polished floor.

His wife approached to see if he was ok, but other than being scared and shaken, all he wanted to do was go home. He certainly didn't want to go back in that house. He mumbled to his wife that something evil had taken over him; he had never felt such hatred in his life and had wanted to cause harm. His wife took him home and the rest of the family went to stay with a relative.

Later, several neighbours who had witnessed the event described a dog – but not a normal dog. It was larger and moved differently, scurrying around as if trying to get to safety. Like a half-man half-dog. When the rest of the family had poured out into the street, it had vanished without a trace.

An artist's impression of a demon. (Authors' collection)

Hearing of the incident, Mr Evans visited the family to perform a second blessing on the house – only this time he brought the Bishop of Worksop and an exorcist with him. He asked the family to stand in a circle whilst he performed a further sanctification on the property. Saying that his work was done, he requested to see the family member who had been possessed by the evil force. However, he was told that the man had been admitted to hospital. Mr Evans, the bishop and the exorcist went straight to Barnsley Hospital and performed a blessing on him also; Mr Evans then told the doctor who was treating him to 'believe everything this man tells you'. Not long after these horrifying events the family moved out, leaving the unknown entity behind.

There are several demons that take the form of a jackal – is this what the family saw? In our opinion, this story has all the traits of a demonic attack!

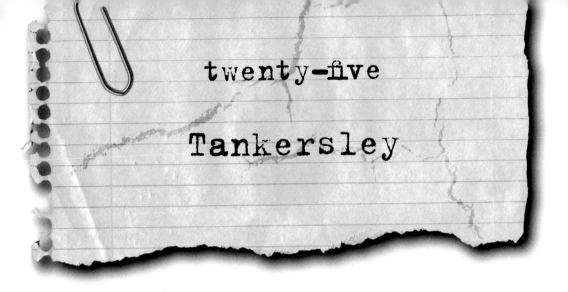

twenty-five

Tankersley

Tankersley Moor

Phantom soldiers have been seen on numerous occasions on Tankersley Moor, the scene of a long-forgotten skirmish. A couple parked their car one night near the old battlefields. Whilst they were sat talking, they saw a figure wandering around in the trees in the shadows of the moonlight. After several minutes, the figure started to walk closer and closer to their car. A little scared, the driver turned on the headlights and was surprised to see a soldier standing there in his full battle uniform. The figure looked at the couple for several minutes before slowly dissolving.

Tankersley Hall

In 1652, the Wentworth family leased the hall to Royalist Sir Richard Fanshawe. The house served as a main residence for the family until July 1654, when their daughter Anne tragically died and was buried in Tankersley churchyard. Soon after this, they left the house and returned to London. As the Wentworth empire grew in the early eighteenth century, the hall fell into disuse and locals gradually dismantled it for the stone. All that was left of the once grand hall are the ruins that survive today.

Tankersley Hall ruin. (Authors' collection)

Tankerlsey Hotel, the former old hall. (Authors' collection)

A hooded figure has been seen circling the perimeter wall of the old hall. It is said to be the restless soul of Anne, searching for her family.

Tankersley Manor Hotel

Today, the seventeenth-century building is a modern hotel, but with many original features retained. Some of the rooms still have the original oak beams and Yorkshire stone window sills.

There have been numerous sightings of a woman sitting in one of the windows, looking out on to the grounds. She is described as wearing a long white gown. When staff investigate the room, she is nowhere to be seen. On other occasions she has been seen from inside the building and has been mistaken for a bridesmaid or bride. Upon being spoken to she simply disappears.

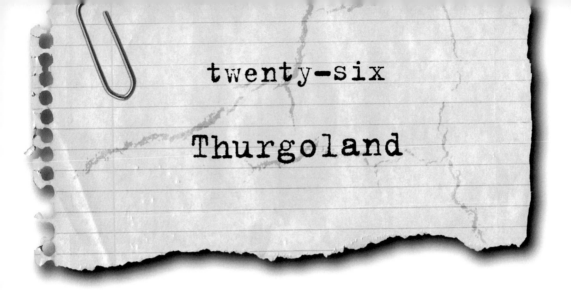

twenty-six

Thurgoland

Hollin Moor Lane and Badger Wood Road

In September 1992, a taxi driver from Kendray was driving home with his wife and their three children. As they came along the back lane between Thurgoland and Hood Green, a ghostly figure floated out towards their car near the Eastfield Inn. They saw what they described as a ghostly outline resembling a man dressed in an old policeman's cape. The featureless shape glided in through the passenger side and right through the bonnet, stalling the engine and grinding them to a halt before drifting off into the woodlands on the other side of the road.

The couple looked at each other in amazement. The taxi driver had seen the strange spectre before, but hadn't dared say anything to anyone through fear of ridicule. However, after reporting the incident to the police, the family were shocked to discover that it was the second report the police had received that night.

Many believe that the ghost is that of a famous inventor, Joseph Bramah, whose workshops once stood on the site. The now homeless spirit is said to wander the area after the buildings he once resided in were pulled down. Mr Bramah was the inventor of the hydraulic press, the beer pump, and the U-bend on toilets. There is a memorial to him in Silkstone Church, where his skills, eminence, benevolence and steadfast Christian faith are all praised.

Jack In Irons

Jack in Irons is a giant of Yorkshire lore who haunts the lonely roads around Barnsley. He is said to be between 8 and 10ft tall and is usually described as wearing black robes and chains. He lurks in alleyways and deserted roads, forever in search of his next victim. Jack is thought to be clapped in the irons of his imprisonment and is self-decorated with the heads of his prey. His weapon of choice is a spiked club that will be the fate of anyone who crosses his path.

It is rumoured that Jack was imprisoned by locals, who feared the great strength that he possessed. They plied him with ale until he fell into a drunken stupor and then clapped him in irons. But it wasn't enough to just imprison Jack; soon they set him to work as a slave, digging canals and tunnels. When he escaped, he started taking homicidal revenge, killing anyone who crossed his path. After his death, Jack was condemned to walk the earth looking for the descendants of his captives. His rage, the product of a life of captivity and enslavement, knows no end.

There is a rumour that his grave is at Dalton in Rotherham, at a mill that is no longer standing. The story connected to this site is that a giant once lived in the mill, using the building to grind his human victims into pulp. Could this have been Jack in Irons? Jack was also possibly the inspiration for Ted Hughes' marvellous book *The Iron Man*. The writer was born in Mytholmroyd, but was raised from early childhood in Mexborough, South Yorkshire.

Many sightings of Jack in Irons date back to the early nineteenth century, when he was frequently seen around the moorland of South and West Yorkshire, normally near Tankersley and Oxspring. A farmer travelling home one autumn evening in the late 1800s, after harvesting his crops, saw a giant figure lurch from the trees. It tipped over his cart, spilling his load across the track. The farmer ran home to tell his sons what he had seen, but the family refused to retrieve the horse and cart until the next morning. On arrival, the cart was right end up but the crops had gone!

We thought that sightings of Jack in Irons had died out, until a lorry driver who wished to remain anonymous contacted us after our appeal for stories in the *Barnsley Chronicle*.

One Friday night in December 2010, the driver was heading back to Chapeltown, Sheffield, from Penistone when snow began to set in. He reduced his speed and stayed in high gears to keep his grip on the road. As he travelled along Halifax Road, he became concerned that he wouldn't make it home through the blizzards. Just as he passed the turning for Crane Moor, the visibility got worse – not to mention the road conditions – and that's when he saw what he thought was a stranded motorist in the road at the edge of the woodland. He slowed down, fearing that there might be a stuck car blocking the road. As he approached the man, he wound down his window to ask if he needed help. But as he drew even closer, he noticed that something was amiss. He described the man as thickset and wearing what looked like a hooded donkey jacket. The figure had the appearance of the 1980s wrestler 'Giant Haystacks'. The driver thought to himself, 'Bloody hell, he's a big bloke. I wonder if he's a fellow wagon driver. I hope his lorry hasn't broken down out here, I'll never get home!' Whilst this was running through his head, the figure lumbered towards him.

It was then that he realised the true stature of the man. By the time they drew level they were looking at each other eye to eye, even though the driver was sitting way up in his cab. This would have made the figure at least 9ft tall. Stunned at the sheer magnitude of the hulking figure before him, all thoughts of offering help quickly disappeared. Not wanting to stop now, the driver carried on moving at about 15mph. Suddenly, the giant figure raised his mighty right arm in what looked like a bid to halt the vehicle. It was only then that the man noticed the large links of iron chain hanging from the figure's wrists. Trying to rationalise what he was seeing, he quickly looked in the mirror, only to see the giant vanish into the blizzard. As he continued his journey, the driver noticed that the figure hadn't left any footprints in the snow.

Jack in Irons, who is often described in legend. (Authors' collection)

'Poor Old Jack in Irons'

On the moors of Yorkshire
When the moon is full and bright
The fog rolls over the county
To hide the evils of the night

On such intrepid evenings
Folk will caution well
Strangers not to venture
Onto the hills of hell
For they will see the Jack in Irons
But will not live to tell

You won't see him coming
But you will surely hear
Clank and clink of his irons
That will grip you in his fear

No man knows where he comes from
Nor to where he goes
And no man who ever crossed him
Arose from the giant's blows

But it's not old Jack that is to blame
But those who clapped him in the chain
For all the bodies that he does lay slain
They're the ones that drove him insane

He lies in wait on lonely roads
Daubs his chains with skulls and bones
Looking for his bloody revenge
He'll get them all in the end!

Paul Wesley, from Doncaster

Fearing ridicule, the driver had never spoken of the event until he saw our request that mentioned the Jack in Irons story. Finally, he gave us his account, on the understanding that we would not release his name or the name of the haulage company that he works for. Our greatest thanks go to him for sharing this sighting with us and entrusting us never to disclose his identity.

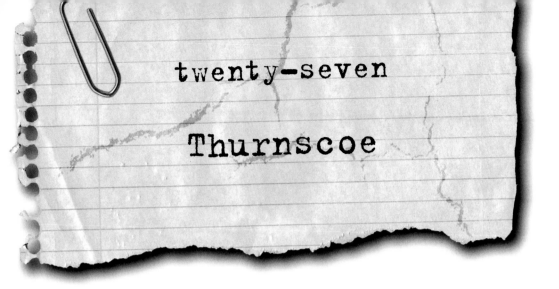

twenty-seven

Thurnscoe

The Thurnscoe Ghoul Train

Local rumour has it that at the top end of Thurnscoe is a disused train line. It is said that if you walk along the bank on your own at night, a ghost train will come along the tracks. The carriages are said to be filled with ghosts and ghouls, who wail and gnash their teeth in perpetual torment, trying to drag others onto the train. Witnesses hear their cries as they disappear into the night.

Cromwell's Cavalry

The following story was sent to us by a man who experienced a strange incident in 2009. We were asked to withhold the man's real name so, for the purpose of this story, we will refer to him as John.

John was out walking one summer's evening. Dusk was approaching so he decided to cut through the fields where Spry Woods are located, so he could head towards Challenger Woods. This was a route John had taken many times before and he had never encountered any strange activity. Just as John got to the stile separating the fields, he stopped and leant over the fence to take a breather. Whilst looking out over Shortwood Lane and Challenger Woods, he saw a bright light heading towards him. At first he thought it was farm machinery, but there was no engine noise coming from it. He stood watching for a moment and realised that it was getting closer and closer. All of a sudden the light seemed to change direction and point away from him, enabling John to see the true source of the light.

Right before him were six Cromwellian soldiers in full uniform. He described them as wearing mustard yellow jackets and full headgear. The front rider stopped his horse and the rest followed suit. He stood up on his stirrups and looked towards John; the stare seemed to last minutes rather than seconds, as John's heartbeat got faster and faster. Then, as if the front soldier had real-

A depiction of Cromwellian soldiers. (Courtesy of Barnsley Reference Library)

ised that John wasn't a threat, he sat back on his horse and, with a hand gesture, commanded the others to follow him. John stood frozen to the spot as the soldiers galloped into the distance before disappearing, as if riding back into their own time. Pulling himself round, and still shaken, he headed for the road, where he felt safe and went home.

John had not spoken about this incident until he saw our request for ghost stories in a local paper. He shared his story to see if anyone else had witnessed anything similar on the same field.

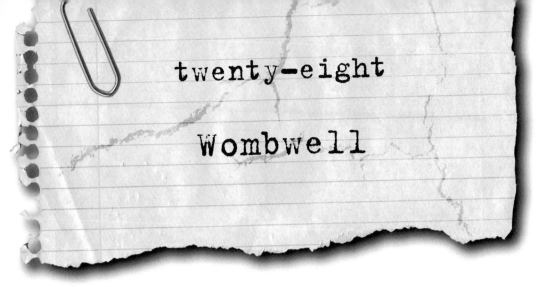

twenty-eight

Wombwell

Shop on High Street (Undisclosed)

The Rotherham Paranormal team were called to this location by the owner of the property, who stated that they were experiencing strange phenomena during trading hours, such as black balls of light appearing from the cellar, people being touched and their clothes being pulled while in the shop, and strange noises. Moreover, footsteps could often be heard walking around in the empty sealed-off rooms upstairs.

The exact age of the building is unknown, but the owners believe that it was built around the eighteenth century. There have been a lot of structural changes since this time, including the second floor and attic space being completely sealed off from the rest of the building. There is also a bricked-up area in the cellar, and the owner always felt that the space behind the wall hid something that shouldn't be found.

During our investigation in the cellar, we heard a man's voice shouting, 'Get out!' This was witnessed by four people. The voice seemed to come from the bricked-up room. Several other EVPs (Electronic Voice Phenomena) were recorded that evening, all similar, making this one of the strangest investigations we have ever conducted.

Wombwell Woods

Wombwell Woods is an ancient woodland that today attracts many visitors. However, it seems to hold a secret. In 1964 a couple were travelling back to Wombwell after a night out in Barnsley. As they turned into the road that runs alongside Wombwell Woods, a man jumped out in front of their car. The driver had no time to stop and drove straight through him. They pulled up to check if he was alright, but soon realised that there had been no impact noise or any damage to the car. The couple have described the man as being tall and wearing dark clothing with a cape, resembling Guy Fawkes. Just before driving through him, the man had swung the cape around his face as if to hide his identity. It is unknown who that man was, or why his ghost haunts the road.

Convicts' Tunnels

During the 1800s, convicts being transported between various Yorkshire courts and prisons often camped in the fields around the tunnels. Due to treacherous paths and weather conditions, many of the weaker prisoners would die en route.

Several ghost sightings have been reported around this area, including the figure of a man running and hiding in the hedgerow. Some believe that he is a prisoner who escaped but later died of exposure. Lone walkers have heard the sounds of footsteps running up behind them, but, as they turn around, the footsteps stop. In addition, local legend says that if you stand in the tunnel at midnight, you hear the sound of a train hurtling towards you, and then feel a gush of wind as it passes you by.

Wombwell Foundry

Wombwell Foundry closed in May 2003 after more than 100 years of production. When the foundry was still in use, a group of night-shift workers claimed to see a shrouded black figure with a stick, kicking up dust in the premises. When chased, the figure simply disappeared into thin air. The figure was seen on many occasions and the men who saw it always tell the same story. It is unknown who the figure was, but we wonder if it will show up again when the land is back in use.

Convicts Tunnel, where strange sounds, including footsteps and a train, have been heard. (Courtesy of Barnsley Reference LIbrary)

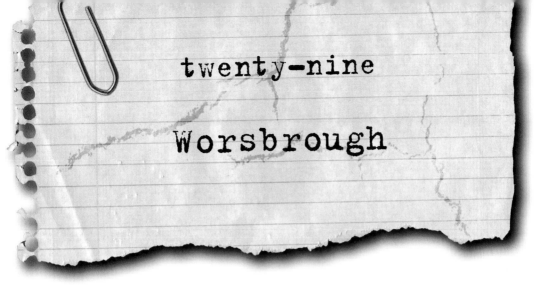

twenty-nine

Worsbrough

Kingswell Woods

During our research for this book, one place kept cropping up: Kingswell Woods. As we dug deeper, we realised that the place has strong connections with the local legend of the Blue Lady. The legend has existed in this area for many years. The Blue Lady, who is believed to have lived at Darley Cliffe Hall around the time of the Civil War, allegedly haunts the ruined turrets in Kingswell Woods in search of her long-lost lover, a Cavalier soldier. A secret room is supposed to exist behind a wall in the wine cellar, and it is whispered that passages lead to the ruined tower and also down the hill-side to nearby St Thomas's Church. The family silver is believed to have been hidden in the tunnels to avoid it being seized by Parliamentary forces. At night, the lady would light a candle and place it in the window, signalling to her lover and his troops that the coast was clear. They would then make their way to the hall through the tunnel to seek refuge.

Roundheads often patrolled the area, knowing that the residence had links with the Marquis of Rockingham, who was loyal to King Charles I. One night the Roundheads stormed the tunnel when the signal was given, expecting to find the loot, but instead they were met by the Lady of the Manor, who was slain in the skirmish. Many years later, a group of men entered the tunnels in search of the treasure, but were scared off by the sound of marching. They were so terrified that they sealed off the entrance and vowed never to let anyone go down there again.

In the summer of 1963, Bill and his friends headed down to the Kingswell Woods late one afternoon. They set off down Sheffield Road and cut across what was locally known as the daisy fields. The sun was just setting over the horizon, silhouetting the trees against a brilliant orange skyline. At that time, Darley Cliffe Hall was dilapidated and unkempt, but the track up to it was well-walked by locals.

The tower that stands on top of the cliff where the ghost of a woman is seen. (Authors' collection)

Just as Bill and his friends approached the wall where the two turrets stand in the woods, they saw a woman emerging from the ruins; it looked like she was wearing a hood. Against the backdrop of the woodland the woman seemed to be glowing, as if she was emitting her own blue light. The group fell silent and stopped in their tracks as they watched the figure glide from behind the wall and make its way across to the other turret. What scared them the most is that the figure would have been walking 50ft in the air, as on the other side of the wall is a sheer drop down the cliff into an old quarried area. They watched the figure in disbelief as it seemed to enter the second tower, and they ran to have a look. When they got to the ruin, the figure had vanished out of sight.

This was not the only story we received regarding the hauntings of Kingswell Woods. One local resident said, 'I haven't been there since 1993, but the memories of the place still scare me … I saw the Blue Lady, nearly causing me to fall to my death. Also, many of my old school friends have seen the ghost-like figure at both of the castles.'

One evening in 2003, three young girls were out in the woods. It was getting dark as they walked across the cinder path between the two towers, along the edge of the cliffs. Suddenly they heard the sound of rustling coming from the furthest tower. They didn't think anything of it at first but the rustling became footsteps, as if someone was following them, and then got louder as if it was giving chase. The girls started to run, too petrified to look behind them. However, the last girl fearfully looked over her shoulder. She saw a big blue outline gliding from the first tower towards them – and then she fell down a ravine. She screamed to her friends, but by the time they'd come to her aid, the figure had gone. Despite her cuts and bruises, the girl was quick to exit the woods. Today, she says, 'If you think this is rubbish, then go and find out yourself if you dare!'

We have received numerous reports, all of a similar nature, regarding the hauntings of Kingswell Woods. All who have seen the Blue Lady say that she leaves a blue trail behind as she glides across the ground. Her hauntings are widespread, covering Staincross Woods and Wentworth Castle.

Worbrough Mill. (Authors' collection)

But nowhere is she more frequently seen than the ruins in Kingswell Woods. Will this restless soul ever find peace in the arms of her brave Cavalier?

Worsbrough Mill

Worsbrough Mill Museum lies on the southern bank of a picturesque valley, standing proud in all its glory. But when the cold winter nights draw in, cloaking the valley in darkness, unwary travellers beware; the mill looms out of the shadows, its windows looking down like vast, condemning eyes, challenging visitors to enter its doors.

The mill is said to be haunted by a mill-worker who died in a tragic accident; he was caught in the machine workings and was crushed by the gears. His workmates managed to free him and carry him to his home (a small cottage that was situated where the car park is now). Unfortunately, he died on the doorstep before he could say goodbye to his wife and children.

When we visited the museum, staff told us of their eerie encounters with the ghostly miller. Many employees get the unnerving feeling that they are being watched when the millworks are activated for demonstrations. Numerous belts and pulleys whir into action, and the entire building vibrates to the tune of the machinery – but it's not just the mill that is brought back to life. A tall, shadowy figure has frequently been sighted during these demonstrations, drifting in and out of the shadows. The hauntings are so well-known in the area that the museum has embraced the spirit, and every Halloween it offers a ghost walk. If you doubt the reports, dare you venture in?

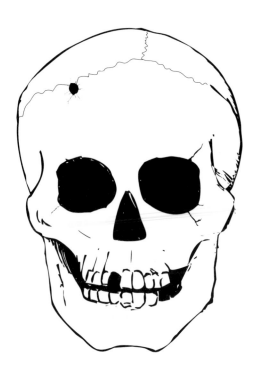

If you enjoyed this book, you may also be interested in ...

Haunted Doncaster
RICHARD BRAMALL & JOE COLLINS

Haunted Doncaster contains a selection of reported ghostly sightings from ordinary people who believe they have had an extraordinary experience. The majority of the locations in this book have been investigated first-hand by the authors, who give the reader an insight into their experience and provide information about the stories behind the alleged sightings. It is sure to appeal to everyone interested in the spectres that inhabit Doncaster's homes, pubs, and highways.

978 0 7524 6375 9

Haunted Rotherham
RICHARD BRAMALL & JOE COLLINS

This fascinating book contains a terrifying collection of true-life tales from in and around Rotherham. Featuring stories such as the Lunatic of Ulley Reservoir and the Old Hag of Hellaby Hall, this pulse-raising compilation of unexplained phenomena, apparitions, poltergeists, curses, spirits and boggards is guaranteed to make your blood run cold.

978 0 7524 6117 5

Haunted Huddersfield
KAI ROBERTS

From heart-stopping accounts of apparitions, manifestations and related supernatural phenomena to first-hand encounters with ghouls and spirits, this collection contains both new and well-known spooky tales and eyewitness accounts from around the West Yorkshire town of Huddersfield. *Haunted Huddersfield* is sure to fascinate everyone with an interest in the town's haunted history.

978 0 7524 6790 0

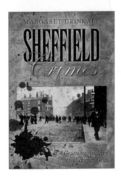

Sheffield Crimes: A Gruesome Selection of Victorian Cases
MARGARET DRINKALL

This volume collects together the most shocking criminal cases from Sheffield's Victorian newspapers. Filled with infamous historical cases - including grave robbing, murder, poisoning, bigamy, and daring jewel and garrotte robberies - and richly illustrated with photographs from private collections and from the local archives. These grisly cases will fascinate residents, visitors and historians alike.

978 0 7524 5820 5

Visit our website and discover thousands of other History Press books.

www.thehistorypress.co.uk